END OF THE LINE

Nancy followed Joe in a leap to the roof of the next car of the speeding train. She saw a look of pure horror pass over his face as he glanced over her shoulder.

"Joe," she asked. "What is it?"

"Look!"

Nancy turned. Coming up—not three hundred yards away—was a tunnel. Frank, still chasing their suspect, had his back to them and the tunnel. There was no way he could know about it.

"Frank!" Nancy and Joe screamed together at the top of their lungs. "Duck!"

It was no use. The roar of the train drowned out their cries. On the last car, Nancy saw Frank make his way along the roof, in hot pursuit of their quarry. She clutched Joe's hand, terrified for Frank.

Then Joe pulled Nancy down flat against the roof of the train. A second later, the darkness of the tunnel surrounded them.

From your friend,
Jessica

Nancy Drew & Hardy Boys SuperMysteries

Available from ARCHWAY Paperbacks

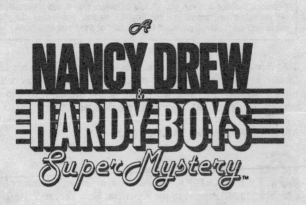

A NANCY DREW & HARDY BOYS Super Mystery™

MYSTERY TRAIN

Carolyn Keene

AN ARCHWAY PAPERBACK
Published by POCKET BOOKS
New York   London   Toronto   Sydney   Tokyo   Singapore

AN ARCHWAY PAPERBACK *Original*

An Archway Paperback published by
POCKET BOOKS, a division of Simon & Schuster Inc.
1230 Avenue of the Americas, New York, NY 10020

Copyright © 1990 by Simon & Schuster Inc.

Produced by Mega-Books of New York, Inc.

ISBN: 0-671-67464-1

First Archway Paperback printing November 1990

10 9 8 7 6 5 4 3 2

NANCY DREW, THE HARDY BOYS, AN ARCHWAY
PAPERBACK and colophon are registered trademarks of
Simon & Schuster Inc.

NANCY DREW & HARDY BOYS SUPERMYSTERY
is a trademark of Simon & Schuster Inc.

Cover illustration by Frank Morris

Printed in U.S.A.

IL 7+

Chapter

One

Nancy!" came Bess Marvin's urgent cry. "Wait for me! We've still got twenty minutes. The train won't leave ahead of schedule."

Nancy Drew's flat shoes slipped on the marble floor of Chicago's Union Station as she stopped quickly and turned to face her friend.

"I know, Bess," she said. "I guess I'm just excited." The light reflecting in Nancy's bright blue eyes danced.

"About seeing Frank and Joe Hardy again?" Bess asked, readjusting her grip on her suitcases and blowing a strand of curly blond hair out of her face.

1

"That. And the whole trip. It's going to be great—" Nancy began.

"Why didn't I wait until after this trip to get my hair permed?" Bess asked, dropping her bags to reach up to fluff out her brand-new ringlets. "Are you sure it looks okay?"

"You look terrific, as usual," Nancy said, reassuring her friend. She scanned the inside of the cavernous building. There was a crowd of people forming at a gate at the far end of the station.

Nancy pushed her reddish blond hair behind her ears and hefted her overnight bag. She grabbed one of the three suitcases Bess had brought along and trapped it between her arm and body. "I'll take this. Can you manage the other two?"

Bess nodded, and with her free hand Nancy picked up her own suitcase and headed in the direction of the gathering crowd. Bess was right that there was plenty of time, but Nancy didn't want to miss a single minute of the trip.

She had been invited, along with Frank and Joe Hardy, to participate in a mystery train ride from Chicago to San Francisco. Bess was coming along as Nancy's guest. The organizers of the ride had invited detectives or writers who specialized in mysteries. During the trip the guests would all try to figure out a real unsolved crime.

2

Nancy didn't know much more, since the trip's organizers wanted to keep the mystery buffs from doing research that might give them an advantage. Now that the trip was about to begin, she was excited to find out more.

She spotted the Hardy brothers talking to each other off to the side. "Frank! Joe!" she called out.

Frank Hardy turned away from his younger brother to smile at Nancy as she hurried up to them and dropped her bags. His brown eyes twinkling, Frank reached out to give her a hug. "Hey, Nancy," he said, stepping back to look at her in her green turtleneck and short black skirt. "You're looking even better than the last time I saw you."

Nancy found herself blushing. Even though she and Frank were not romantically involved at all, he was still the one guy—besides Ned Nickerson, her boyfriend—who could make her blush.

"You look pretty sharp yourself, Frank," Nancy said. Frank was dressed in chinos and a blue sports shirt, open at the collar.

"What about me?" blond, burly Joe Hardy asked, stretching his arms to give Nancy a bear hug. "It's great to see you, Nancy."

"You, too, Joe," Nancy said, smiling at him. "Isn't this trip a fantastic idea?"

"It would be even better if I hadn't decided

to bring so much junk," Bess moaned, appearing next to them. "I should have listened to you, Nan. Hi, Joe. Hi, Frank." She let her bags crash to the marble floor and gave each of the Hardys a kiss on the cheek.

"Can I have your attention, please?" A tall, blond, fortyish woman in a royal blue suit and a red blouse was addressing the group.

The crowd of about thirty people grew quiet. Nancy watched as the attractive woman with the high cheekbones and aristocratic nose put her hand on the arm of a tall, middle-aged man next to her. "My name is Laurie Adams," the woman said, introducing herself. "And this is my husband, Jack Lerner."

The man cleared his throat. "As you know, Laurie and I organized this trip. We're glad you could all make it. We think we've put together a pretty exciting event."

"Does he mean solving the crime?" Bess asked Nancy in a whisper.

"I'm sure that's what he means," Frank said. "And we're the ones who are going to do it, too. Right, Nancy?"

"I don't know," Nancy said modestly. "From what I've heard there are some heavyweight mystery people here."

"Like who?" Joe wanted to know.

As if in answer to Joe's question, Jack Lerner began addressing the crowd again. "Some of you may know one another or know of one another by reputation. I hope you'll get a chance to meet everyone on the trip. For now let me give a general introduction by saying that some of the best minds in the mystery field are here. Over the next five days you'll have the opportunity to work together—or challenge one another—with your methods."

"Jack and I are proud that you all wanted to take part in solving our mystery," Laurie added.

"Why doesn't she cut the jawing and tell us what the mystery *is?*" a man in a checkered sports jacket and tan pants asked the gray-haired woman standing next to him.

The woman gave him a wan smile. "I think she's about to, sir," she said mildly.

Nancy turned to Frank and lifted an eyebrow. "Looks like people are getting tense," she commented.

"It's not surprising," Frank said. "The reward for solving this case is sizable."

"No kidding—twenty-five thousand dollars," Nancy whispered back.

"I know what I'd do with twenty-five grand," Joe said, a big grin on his face. "Buy a souped-up, customized van."

"We've already got one," Frank pointed out.

"Well, then, we could each have one. How's that?" Joe punched Frank lightly on the arm.

"No way you're going to win, Joe Hardy," said Bess with a glint in her blue eyes. *"I'm* going to crack this case and buy myself an expensive designer dress."

"Is it too much to hope that you'll have enough money left over to treat us all to an expensive designer dinner?" Nancy joked. She turned her attention back to the Lerners, who were passing out large manila envelopes.

"Since I know you are all eager to get started, I'm passing out envelopes that contain everything Jack and I know about the crime you're to solve," Laurie told the crowd. "There's also a map of our route and a description of the crime inside."

"If anybody hasn't received a packet, please see me," Jack said. "I have your room assignments, the keys to your compartments, and name tags for you to wear."

"When does the train leave?" the man in the checkered sports jacket called out, glancing at his watch.

Jack laughed. "As soon as we all get on board. So you might want to wait to look at what's inside the envelopes until you've gotten on the train."

Nancy took the envelope Bess was handing her and watched as people started to line up for their compartment assignments and keys. She decided to wait until the line was shorter.

Besides, she was itching to open the envelope and find out what the mystery was.

"We're on the trail of a stolen diamond!" Bess exclaimed. She'd already ripped her envelope open and was reading the first page from it.

Nancy scanned the handout. "Hey, this looks pretty tough," she commented.

Fifteen years ago, she read, the Comstock Diamond had been stolen from Brigston's Limited, a Chicago auction house. Now the train was going to trace what the Lerners believed was the route of the thief as he moved west to San Francisco.

Oddly enough, the thief's route followed the trail of a miner named Jake Comstock—who was the first owner of the diamond, in the nineteenth century—as he mined for silver and gold.

Frank saw that Nancy looked as puzzled as he felt. "How are we supposed to find the thing?" he asked her, holding up a photocopied map. "The thief went from Chicago to San Francisco. He could have stashed the diamond anywhere along the way."

"Or even taken it with him all the way to San Francisco," Joe pointed out.

"There's no way to be sure," Frank agreed.

"I think we're getting ahead of ourselves," Nancy said. "There's a lot we don't know. Like how the Lerners put the map together. Details of the original crime. Why the thief followed Jake Comstock's route—if he did. What we have here is just the beginning of the mystery."

"And it's our job to get to the end," Bess concluded firmly.

"Right! Let's go." Nancy grabbed her suitcase and helped Bess cart her luggage over to where Jack Lerner was handing out the compartment assignments. Frank and Joe followed close behind.

Most of the group had already gotten their keys and were heading through the gate to the train. Jack had just finished handing over a set of keys to a middle-aged couple and their teenage son. In front of Nancy a short, stocky, dark-haired man with a new beard stepped up to Jack.

Jack's eyes narrowed, as if he knew the man but couldn't quite place him. The man started talking in a low voice to Jack.

Jack listened intently to what the short man was saying. Then he looked at Nancy and her friends. "Excuse me, folks," he said with a smile. "This'll take just a second." He beckoned to the short man, and the two moved a few feet away. The little man began speaking again.

Frank was studying his copy of the route map. "I'm trying to see if there's any pattern to

8

the stops," he said to the others. "Hmm—the first stop is a town called Emerald, in Nebraska."

"Well, we *are* looking for a diamond," Bess said excitedly. "Maybe all the town names are precious stones."

"Nice try, Bess, but the next stop is Central City, Colorado," Joe told her.

Nancy became distracted by the sound of raised voices behind her. She turned and observed the short man and Jack.

"You're not getting rid of me that easily," the little man was insisting.

Jack looked over and caught Nancy's eye. "I'll be right with you," he said, reassuring her before turning his attention back to the man.

"Now—" he began, but Jack didn't have a chance to finish. The short man had grabbed him by his shirtfront. He drew back his fist and let fly with a blow that sent Jack reeling to the ground.

Chapter

Two

"Oof!" Jack Lerner gasped as he landed in a heap.

"Hey!" Joe Hardy took a step toward Jack's assailant. The man shot him a venomous glare before taking off for the gate. Joe and Frank were right behind him.

Nancy dropped to her knees beside Jack. "Are you all right?" He nodded that he was okay, but he looked dazed.

Frank and Joe moved fast, but when they got to the platform, the man was nowhere in sight.

"Rats!" Frank said, shaking his head. He and Joe made their way back up the platform to the gate and station lobby.

"He disappeared," Joe said in response to Nancy's questioning look.

Nancy was helping Jack up. "Did you know that man, Mr. Lerner?" she inquired.

"Er, please—call me Jack," he said, blinking at Nancy. "Did I know that man, you ask?"

"Right."

"Ah." Jack brushed dust off his jacket and pants. "I've never seen him before in my life, but he was very anxious to get on the Mystery Train to San Francisco. When I told him it was a special run, not open to the public, he got—shall we say—upset. Before I knew it, I was staring at his fist."

Nancy shook her head. "I don't see why he got so upset. He could have taken another train," she remarked. "It's weird."

Jack patted his upper lip with a white handkerchief. "You're telling me," he said.

Bess's eyes were round. "Are you sure you're okay?" she asked.

Lerner smiled. "It hurts," he said with a small laugh, putting his hand to his lip, "but I'll be fine." He smoothed back his graying hair and picked up the papers that had gone flying. Finally he turned to the four teenagers.

"I'm sorry," he said, looking contrite. "I haven't thanked you—or asked who you all are."

Frank reached out to shake Jack's hand.

"Frank Hardy," he said. "This is my brother, Joe, and that's Nancy Drew and Bess Marvin."

"Of course," said Jack. He let go of Frank's hand and shook Nancy's. "In Chicago we often hear about the famous teenage detective Nancy Drew. You're from River Heights, right?"

"Yes, I am," Nancy replied. She was a little embarrassed. She knew that her name was pretty well known in some circles, but she wasn't famous. Jack was exaggerating.

Jack turned his attention back to the Hardys. "I hear that you boys are also quite the sleuths."

Frank smiled awkwardly. "Joe and I have solved a few cases—it's true," he said modestly.

"We've all worked together, too," Bess put in. "Just last spring Nancy, Frank, Joe, and I caught a famous art smuggler in Paris."

"That's terrific," Jack said brightly. "I'd love to hear about it sometime. Right now, though—"

"Right now, though, I say we get our keys and stow our stuff on board," Joe chimed in.

Jack nodded, peering at his watch. "That little scene put us a bit behind schedule. I'm sure Laurie is wondering what's holding us up."

He checked a list and handed Frank two keys and two name tags. "You and your brother are sharing a compartment. And Nancy, I've put you and Bess together."

Nancy took the keys and name tags from Jack. "Let's find our compartments," she said to Frank. "I want to settle in and get a chance to read all the materials before dinner."

Frank led the way through the gate and down the empty platform. Through the train's windows Frank could see the other guests settling into their compartments.

A porter standing near the train checked Frank's key and gave him directions to the second-to-last sleeper car. Nancy and Bess's compartment was close to Frank and Joe's.

"There'll be an informal meeting in the dining car at five," Jack said, moving up to join them. "See you all there."

Frank nodded and led the way through the train to their car.

"Here we are," Nancy said, stopping at the first compartment. "Hey, Bess, we've got a suite," she said as she opened the door.

"See you in the dining car at five?" Frank asked, checking his watch.

"You bet," said Nancy.

As Frank and Joe headed down the narrow, carpeted corridor toward their suite, Frank felt the train begin to jerk forward.

"All right!" cheered Joe. "We're on our way."

The Hardys' compartment was smaller than Nancy and Bess's. There were two seats facing each other that slid together to make a bed, and a bunk that pulled down above one of the seats.

Frank tossed his bag and settled into one of the seats. He pulled down a tray from against the wall. "Top or bottom?" he asked absently as he opened his envelope.

"Top." Joe sat down across from Frank. "Do you think Jack knew the guy who punched him?"

"He says he didn't. Hard to tell from the way they were talking," said Frank. He studied the map of their route. "It looks like we're stopping at mostly mining towns," he said a little later.

"That's because Jake Comstock was a forty-niner who went west with the gold rush," Joe reminded his brother.

"Why do Jack and Laurie think the thief followed Jake's route?" Frank mused.

"I guess we'll have to ask Jack and Laurie," Joe said, stretching and looking at his watch. "It's almost five."

Frank picked up his papers, grabbed a pen and a pad, and put on his name tag. "Let's go."

By the time Frank and Joe made it to the dining car, Nancy and Bess were already there.

Nancy waved them over to their table. Around them the other members of the group were quietly talking.

Nancy held up the envelope of information. "This mystery has so few clues, it's hard to know where to begin," she commented.

Jack Lerner called for their attention. "I hope you've all had a chance to read the handouts, and if you have I'm sure you have some questions."

"Tell us what you know about the original owner," a woman on Frank's right called out in a commanding voice. Her name tag read "Maggie Horne."

"That's not *the* Maggie Horne, is it?" Frank whispered to the others. The wispy gray hair and blue eyes seemed familiar. Maybe from a photograph on a book's dust jacket or one in a magazine about mystery writers, Frank decided.

"It must be," Nancy said, studying the woman. "I heard there were going to be famous people here, but Maggie Horne is the queen of American mystery writers!"

"Shhh," Bess whispered. "I want to hear what Jack is saying."

"As some of you may know, the Comstock Diamond is very unusual. It's a beautiful gem. The most striking thing about it is its cut—a

15

simple pyramidal shape. But it's not a fabulously expensive diamond—it's not flawless. Its history as the Comstock Diamond is what makes it important."

"Mmm. I'll take it," Bess murmured.

"Its original owner was a successful miner turned rich banker, Jake Comstock," Jack went on. "After Comstock's death, the diamond disappeared—he had hidden it and hadn't told anyone where. Years later the last of the San Francisco Comstocks died, and the contents of the Comstock mansion were auctioned off. Some of the goods ended up at Brigston's auction house in Chicago, and in that lot was a box that contained the Comstock Diamond. So it had come to light at last—only to be stolen from Brigston's almost immediately," Jack continued.

Laurie took up the story. "Brigston's has sponsored this trip and put up the reward. A Brigston's representative is aboard to oversee the trip—her name is Sara Finney. She can tell you what they know about the theft. Sara?"

A pretty brown-haired young woman with hazel eyes stood up from a table near Jack and Laurie. She smoothed the skirt of her houndstooth check suit and gave the crowd a smile. "I'm sorry that there's not much to tell," she said. "Fifteen years ago the diamond was stolen from Brigston's, the night before it was to be auctioned. It was locked in a vault with other valuable items, none of which was touched. Whoever took the Comstock Diamond seems to have been after it and it alone.

"We believe only one burglar committed the actual break-in," she went on, "although it's possible that he—or she—had one or more accomplices. It was a professional job—the security system was turned off, the guards knocked out, and no fingerprints were left."

"Did the police come up with any clues?" Frank asked.

Sara shook her head. "No. The only thing we know is that the job was done by a pro."

"What did Brigston's do?" Nancy put in.

"The auction house followed its usual procedures—a full investigation, offers of a reward, and so on," Sara told the group. "But we reached a dead end—or the auction house did. I wasn't with them at the time."

"Why did you decide to reopen the case after all this time?" a man in the crowd asked. Frank recognized him as the guy in the checkered sports jacket.

Jack spoke up. "About three years ago Ralph Machlin, one of the regulars at Jimmy's—for those of you who may not know, that's the restaurant Laurie and I own," he interrupted himself. "Anyway, Machlin started doing research into the theft for a book he was writing about unsolved crimes in Chicago. The map you have was drawn up by Machlin—it's his research."

"Machlin!" the man in the checkered jacket practically shouted. "Why, that guy was washed up! If this map is Machlin's, we might as well turn this train around and head back to Chicago."

Several people in the crowd drew in their breath at once. Frank saw Maggie Horne give the guy a chilly stare. "I don't think that kind of comment is appropriate," she said in a cold voice. "Just who are you to say it, anyway?"

"My name's Conrad Everett, but you can all call me Connie," the guy said, standing up and facing the crowd. "Sorry to offend you, Ms. Horne, but I knew Ralph Machlin, and I'm telling you the guy's research was always full of holes."

Frank raised an eyebrow at his brother. "This is getting interesting," he said.

Laurie spoke up. "Ralph Machlin was a good man. I'd rather we didn't discuss him, since he's not here to defend himself."

"Where is he?" Frank asked.

"He died last year," Connie put in. He jabbed a finger at the Lerners. "Hey, how'd you two get hold of his papers, anyway? I was his friend, and he never handed over any of his notes to *me*."

"With friends like you, who needs enemies?" someone in the crowd muttered.

Laurie's expression told everyone how uncomfortable she felt. "Please, let's try to keep this friendly." She leaned forward to talk to Everett. "Ralph and I used to talk a lot. Shortly before he died, he gave me the Comstock research to look over. He was very excited about it and hoped to take a trip along this route himself to see what he could verify. In a way I look at this trip as sort of a vindication of his work. He had some bad breaks in his last years, you know."

"That's very touching. We'll just have to find out for ourselves if Mr. Machlin knew what he was doing or not, won't we?" Maggie Horne asked with authority.

Several people nodded and gave Connie Everett hard stares.

Laurie cleared her throat. "Thank you. And now, moving right along—Kate? Paul? Would you stand up, please?"

Following Laurie's gaze, Frank turned in his seat to see a young couple standing at the back of the car. The woman was tall and willowy, with red hair and green eyes. The man had straight blond hair and brown eyes—the kind of good looks Frank associated with soap opera actors.

"He's gorgeous!" Bess said breathily.

"These two young people are Kate Harkins and Paul Fox," Jack explained. "They're actors and singers who sometimes help us out at Jimmy's with our mystery dinners. We make up a crime with suspects and then have our patrons try to solve it. Kate and Paul are going to entertain us a little on the trip."

Kate and Paul smiled at the crowd and waved before sitting down. Frank glanced over at his brother to confirm that Joe's eyes would be riveted on Kate. They were.

Nancy tapped Frank's shoulder and moved her head in Bess's direction. Frank saw that Bess was also in another world—Paul Fox's, to be exact.

"At least *we* still have our minds on the mystery," Frank joked.

Nancy laughed. "Someone has to."

Joe turned around to face his brother at the same moment that Bess took her eyes off Paul. "What did you say?" they asked in unison.

"Nothing," Frank answered. "Nancy and I were just discussing the mystery."

"Oh," Joe said absently, standing up. "We've got some time before dinner." He paused awkwardly. "I thought I might—"

Frank finished for him. "Get Kate Harkins's autograph?"

Joe shrugged and stepped away from the table. "She'd probably get a kick out of it. I doubt she's famous or anything."

"I'll go with you, Joe," said Bess, grabbing her purse. "I want to ask Paul Fox what it's like to act in mysteries. It might help with our case," she added weakly.

"Sure, sure," said Nancy. "Frank and I will stay right here." She grinned at Frank.

Joe left them with a relieved sigh. "It's not as if we're going to stop working on the case," Joe said to Bess.

"Of course not," Bess said, reassuring him. "We care too much about solving the mystery. We just want to, uh, meet Kate and Paul and say hi and make them feel welcome."

There was a small crowd around the actors. Joe stood by patiently while Kate answered questions. Bess was bolder. She walked right up to Paul Fox, fluffing her blond curls and smiling flirtatiously.

Finally Kate moved away from the crowd, and Joe got up the nerve to approach her. He wasn't usually shy, so he didn't know why he felt that way suddenly. Except maybe it was because Kate's green eyes were so beautiful—

Then, in an instant, he was standing next to her and staring down into those beautiful eyes.

"Hi," he said. "My name's Joe Hardy."

"Hi, Joe," said Kate. Was it his imagination, or did her voice suddenly become softer?

"I'd like to talk to you sometime. About—" About what? Joe wondered.

"How about now?" Kate asked. "We have some time before dinner. But if you don't mind, I'd like to get some fresh air while we talk. Isn't there an observation deck or something?"

Yes! Joe could hardly hold back his grin. The Hardy charm wasn't lost at all. It was still working on high power. "I bet there's a fantastic view from the back of the train. Would you like to check it out?"

Kate's face lit up. "Sure. I think trains are neat, don't you? To me, it's the best way to travel. A lot more relaxing than planes."

"You know, you're right," Joe said, leading the way through the dining car toward the back of the train. "My brother and I travel a lot by plane because we don't have time for trains. And, of course, you can't take a train to Europe, which we do a lot. Go to Europe, that is."

He winced as soon as the words were out of his mouth. Wow, was that a dumb thing to say! That weird shyness was coming over him again.

He led Kate down the corridor of the last

sleeper car. "Here we are," he said, pointing out the very obvious door at the back of the train. He almost blushed.

"Why do you and your brother go to Europe a lot?" Kate asked him.

Joe struggled with the handle of the door. It wouldn't turn! Finally he realized he was supposed to pull the handle toward him. Rolling his eyes, he got it open.

"We're detectives," he said, holding the door for Kate. "We go all over the world to solve mysteries." Oh, boy, does that sound conceited or what? he groaned to himself.

A rush of brisk early-evening air greeted them. As Kate stepped out onto the small platform, her red hair was blown straight back from her face by the breeze. "This was a great idea!" she shouted over the clatter of the train's wheels.

Joe stepped out to stand next to her, and Kate turned to face him. She leaned against a safety chain that ran from one end of the small platform to the other.

"So what did you want to talk about?" she asked.

Joe was about to make something up when the train suddenly lurched. Kate reached out to steady herself by grabbing the chain. In a flash her green eyes went wide.

"Joe!" she cried. "I'm falling!"

Chapter

Three

THE CHAIN Kate was holding came loose at one end and flew over the edge of the platform. The actress started to follow it out over the rails.

Without thinking, Joe threw himself at the redhead and grabbed her around the waist. He yanked her back onto the platform, and both of them fell flat—Joe almost on top of Kate.

They lay there winded and dazed until Kate caught her breath and spoke first. "Oh, Joe," she said. "I thought it was over." She looked over at him with huge, scared green eyes.

Feeling suddenly awkward, Joe hopped to

his feet and reached down to help Kate up. "Hey, I wouldn't have let that happen to you."

Kate brushed the hair out of her face and gave him a weak smile. "I'm lucky you have such quick reflexes," she said. "It must be because of the dangerous work you do."

Joe shrugged, feeling embarrassed. "Let's see just what happened here," he said, stepping past her and moving toward the edge of the platform.

The chain was still dangling off the end of the platform. The metal rings struck the rails every few seconds, sending out showers of sparks. Joe pulled the chain up toward him. The last metal loop that had been linked to the iron railing along the train's platform was rusted and broken off.

"It snapped right off," Joe concluded. "You probably loosened the last link when you leaned against the chain. Then, when the train lurched and you grabbed the chain, the link broke completely."

Kate studied the chain. "Boy," she said, swallowing hard. "I really was lucky."

"Try not to think about it," Joe suggested. "Maybe we should stick to safer places the next time we want to check out the view."

"Like the observation deck?" Kate suggested with a laugh.

"Right." Joe pushed the door in and held it open for Kate.

She smiled at him as she brushed by. "There are a lot of questions I'd like to ask you sometime about what it's like to be a detective." She started down the long tunnellike corridor, swaying from side to side in rhythm to the train's steady rocking motion.

"What do you want to know?" Joe asked, keeping up with her.

"What it feels like to be in danger, for one," she said.

"That's a question you should be able to answer now," Joe said, referring to her near mishap.

Kate laughed, and Joe admired the gentle, sweet sound she made.

"Have you been acting a long time?" Joe asked. "I mean, you look pretty young."

"I'm twenty, but I've been acting since I was in high school," Kate told him. "My parents wanted me to go to college, but I decided to try acting instead. It's hard to break in, but I know I'll make it."

Joe sensed the determination in her voice. "I'm sure you will," he said, and meant it.

"Kate!" a man's voice called out. "I've been looking all over for you. Where were you?"

Over Kate's shoulder Joe saw Paul Fox heading toward them. From the look on Paul's face

Joe could tell the actor wasn't happy to see him.

"We went for a walk," Kate said in a vague tone. "I—I wanted to stretch my legs."

"That's nice," Paul said. "If you're finished with your tour, Jack and Laurie would like to see you."

"I'm coming to see them right now, at dinner," Kate said.

"Hey, why don't you both have dinner with me and my friends?" Joe put in, trying his best to be polite to the actor.

Paul scowled. "Some other time. We're eating with Jack, Laurie, and Sara Finney."

Kate looked at Joe. "Thanks for the invitation, though. Could we have breakfast tomorrow?"

"I'd like that," Joe said.

"If you two have finished making a date, Kate and I have to be leaving," Paul said abruptly. "Kate?"

"Tomorrow, then," Kate said, giving Joe one last look before following Paul.

Nice guy, Joe thought. He wondered what he'd done to upset Paul so much. Maybe it was just that Paul felt protective toward Kate.

Or maybe the two of them were going out. That thought hadn't occurred to Joe until just then. He discovered he didn't like it.

* * *

Nancy was sitting with Bess and Frank at a table in the dining car when Joe walked in.

"Joe looks kind of glum," she said to Frank. "I wonder if something happened with Kate."

Frank's eyes followed Joe as he walked toward them. "I'll try to find out."

Bess looked up from her menu, not having followed the conversation at all. "All I know is, Paul Fox has to be the dreamiest guy I've seen since—"

"Since yesterday?" Nancy joked.

"Very funny, Nancy," said Bess. "You know it's been ages since I've gone with anyone."

"I know, Bess," Nancy said, taking a sip of her water. "I'm only teasing." Bess's boy-craziness never ceased to amaze Nancy.

"Are you okay?" Frank asked Joe after he sat down.

Joe, whose eyes were focused down the car on Kate Harkins, took them off her long enough to answer. "Sure, I'm fine. I just hope Kate is. We had a little accident just now, and I hope she's not too shook up."

"What happened?" Frank asked.

They all listened as Joe told them about how Kate had nearly fallen off the train. "I have to let Jack know about that chain as soon as dinner is over," Joe added.

"You should," Nancy said. "You're lucky something more serious didn't happen."

Joe nodded. "I know. What's for dinner?" he asked, changing the subject.

Nancy could tell Joe was still pretty shaken as she picked up her menu. "We seem to have a choice of steak, pasta, or chicken." There were boxes down one side of the menu, and Nancy watched as the guests at another table checked off their choices. Waiters were passing through the car, serving salads and picking up the cards.

"This is a pretty neat system," Bess said, handing their waiter her card. "Do you recognize many of these people, Nancy?" she asked later during a lull in the conversation.

"A few." Nancy scanned the crowd. She noticed a tall man seated next to Maggie Horne. "Isn't that John Gryson—you know, the guy who played Sherlock Holmes in that TV movie last month?"

Bess turned in her chair. "You're right!" she said. "Wow! John Gryson. I heard he's got a new movie coming out soon. A thriller."

Frank dug into his salad. "Just before dinner Jack told me that the guy who wrote the screenplay for Gryson's movie is here, too."

"That must be him sitting at Gryson's table," Joe said. "The short guy with the glasses and the weird-looking tie."

"That's him," Nancy said, glancing discreetly at Maggie Horne's table again. "That's Lee

Goldstein. He used to be a science-fiction writer before he started writing mysteries. His latest mystery's on the best-seller list right now, in fact."

"Since when do you know so much about him?" Bess asked Nancy.

"Since I started reading *Mystery Scene,*" Nancy told her.

"You have to keep busy somehow between cases, right, Nancy?" Frank said with a smile. He pushed his salad away to make room for the steak the waiter was putting in front of him.

"Mmm, this looks great!" said Bess as the waiter served her her chicken.

"Frank reads *Forensic Medicine Today* for fun. It's not what I'd call great light reading," Joe said, grinning at his brother.

"What is forensic medicine?" Bess wanted to know.

Frank swallowed a mouthful of steak. "Mainly it's the study of murder victims' bodies. It sounds creepy, but I really learn a lot by reading about it."

"I think I'll stick to car magazines," said Joe. He twirled his pasta around his fork and took a bite. "And the occasional comic book, of course."

"Forensic medicine, huh? I think I just lost my appetite," Bess murmured.

"Great! Pass me your plate," Joe suggested.

Bess slapped his hand away. "Hands off, Joe Hardy! I think I'm feeling better already."

The four friends ate in silence for a few minutes, and Nancy took that opportunity to look around the dining car for Connie Everett. She wanted to talk to him after dinner about what made him so sure Machlin's research was flawed. If what Everett said was even partly true, their trip could really be a wild-goose chase.

"Earth to Nancy," said Bess. The waiter was clearing their plates. "Are you finished?"

Nancy put her napkin on the table beside her plate. "I guess I wasn't that hungry," she said.

"I was. I've still got room for some of that chocolate mousse cake," Joe said.

"Tea for me," Frank told the waiter.

"The same," said Nancy.

Bess looked thoughtful for a minute, then sneaked a glance at Paul Fox. "Same for me, too," she said. "I'd hate to have Paul see me pigging out on cake. He might get the wrong idea."

Nancy laughed and leaned back in her chair. "I was thinking of talking to Connie Everett after dinner," she said. "Do any of you want to help me check out what he meant by those remarks about Ralph Machlin?"

31

Joe nodded. "Sounds good," he said. "How about you, Frank?"

Frank shrugged. "Fine with me."

"Bess?" Nancy asked.

Bess blotted below her left eye—it was tearing, for some reason. Then she took her guide book out of her bag. "Oh, no, thanks, Nancy. I want to read up on our stops, then maybe I'll ask Paul Fox a few questions. Jack and Laurie might have told him something about Jake Comstock and the diamond. It's worth checking out."

Nancy grinned. Bess was so transparent!

The dining car was slowly emptying out, and Nancy still hadn't spotted Connie Everett. "Have any of you seen Everett?" she asked her friends.

Bess shook her head as she started to cough. "No," she managed to say. "Boy, who's the chain smoker in here?"

Nancy's eyes were stinging now, too, and several other passengers were coughing. She whirled around. The car was filling up with smoke.

"Look!" Frank cried, pointing.

Huge waves of smoke were billowing into the car from the car just ahead. Waiters and cooks were coughing and fanning the smoke with towels.

Nancy jumped up from the table, with Frank

and Joe close behind. She pushed her way past the other guests and headed for the smoky car, covering her mouth and nose with her napkin.

One of the waiters saw her coming and blocked her way. "You'd better stay back, miss," he warned. "The kitchen's on fire!"

Chapter

Four

NANCY HEARD SHOUTS coming from the next car. "Is that the kitchen?" she asked the waiter.

He nodded. "But you'd better not go in there. They're trying to put the fire out now."

Nancy turned to Frank and Joe. "I want to see what's going on," she said. She fought her way past the waiter and through the smoke toward the space connecting the two cars.

"Be careful," Frank warned Nancy and his brother.

All three of them had tied their napkins around their faces, and they looked like old-fashioned bank robbers.

Nancy, who was in the lead, called back to Frank and Joe. "I see flames. And there's a lot of smoke."

Just as Nancy reached the kitchen entrance, someone rushed past her, knocking her off balance.

"Hey," she called out. "Watch where you're going!"

Whoever it was didn't stop to apologize. She heard Frank and Joe shout as the man pushed his way past them, too.

The kitchen was in chaos. One of the cooks had a fire extinguisher in his hands and was shouting at a short, dark-haired woman to get out of his way. He aimed the fire extinguisher at a stove and sent out a blast of foam. Flames licked up for a second, nearly scorching the ceiling. Then there was a sizzling sound as the foam started blanketing the fire.

"It was that guy, I'm telling you!" the dark-haired woman was shouting at the cook with the extinguisher. "The stocky, short one who just ran out of here. I saw him doing something with a can of motor oil a few minutes ago."

The cook ignored the woman, but Nancy didn't. She shouted above the noise. "What guy?"

The woman pointed at the door behind Nancy. "He probably ran right past you. I tried to stop him, but he got by me."

"Who?" Frank wanted to know. He was standing next to Nancy now.

"The guy who pushed his way past us," Nancy guessed.

"I don't know where he came from," the woman said. "He just showed up, and the next thing I knew, the whole stove was on fire. He must have done it."

"Let's go!" Joe shouted. He raced off with Frank and Nancy right after him.

In the dining car the few remaining guests were milling around. One man was standing alone and stock-still. When he saw Nancy, he took off, vanishing through the far door.

"There he is!" Nancy shouted to Frank, who took up the chase with Joe.

When Nancy caught up to the Hardys, their quarry was in the middle of the lounge car, heading toward a sleeper car.

"We can't lose him now!" she told them urgently. "I think he's the same guy who punched Jack back at the station."

"I was thinking the same thing," Frank said, opening the door to the sleeper car. Nancy charged through first.

The man was lurching from side to side down the narrow aisle toward the next sleeper car. For one brief moment he turned around, and Nancy got a look at him. He seemed to be in his midthirties, with black hair shot through with gray. A scruffy growth of beard gave his face a tough edge.

Nancy caught his eye for a moment, and the look he gave her through narrowed eyes was dark and threatening. In the next second he had turned around and quickened his pace.

"It's the same guy, all right. Where do you think he's going?" Nancy asked over her shoulder.

"He's got to know he's trapped," Frank said.

"Unless there's some way off this train we don't know about," Joe offered. "Look!"

The man had stopped at the far end of the car and was working to remove an emergency exit window.

Nancy felt a blast of cool air as the culprit yanked the window out of its frame and into the car. "He's going to jump!" she shouted to Frank and Joe.

Frank tore ahead of Nancy and Joe. The man was standing on the window frame—his upper body was outside the window. Frank lunged for his legs, but the short guy was too fast. He kicked back once at Frank, and then his legs disappeared through the window.

Frank wondered where he had gone—he obviously hadn't landed on the ground. The cool night air blew Frank's hair straight back as the countryside whipped past. In the dusky light all he could make out were the rolling hills of eastern Iowa. His quarry wasn't in sight.

Then he spotted the iron ladder bolted onto the train, next to the window. It ran up to the roof of the car.

He twisted around and pointed out the ladder to Nancy and Joe. "He must be on the roof!" he announced. "I'm going after him."

Nancy and Joe exchanged a look. They both knew it was a crazy move. The train was going eighty miles an hour—at least.

Joe squared his shoulders. "Well, I'm sure not letting you go up there alone," he said.

"Me, neither," Nancy added firmly.

Frank was on the ladder now. When he had safely pulled himself up and flattened himself on the roof, Joe followed with Nancy right behind.

Outside the train it was dark and cold. The wind made it hard for Nancy to keep a solid grip, but she held on fast to the ladder and made her way up slowly.

Once she got to the top, Joe was there, kneeling, with a hand out to pull her to safety. Frank still lay flat. Then he got into a half-crouch to look for any sign of their quarry.

"There he is!" Frank cried, pointing toward the rear of the train.

Forty feet and another car away, the culprit

was crawling along the roof in a weaving motion.

Frank took off after him first in a crablike scuttle—hands and feet both on the roof for balance.

"Turn your feet out," Joe told Nancy. "That way you won't slip. And keep low. Put your hands down in front of you. If you don't, the wind will knock you off in a second."

Nancy followed his advice and found she was able to creep along the train's roof. Up ahead she could see Frank steadily gaining on the short, stocky guy.

"He's almost got him!" she shouted to Joe above the roar of the train.

Joe turned back to answer Nancy. "We've got to get closer and help him!" he shouted back.

Nancy nodded and pushed forward. Suddenly she heard a long mournful whistle over her shoulder. A train was coming from the opposite direction, and within seconds she felt a blast of air from the train as it roared past them. The force knocked both her and Joe flat onto the roof of the train.

"Nancy!" Joe cried. "Are you okay?"

Nancy carefully picked herself up. "I'm fine," she managed to say. "How far ahead are they?" She peered into the distance.

"They're on the next car," Joe said. "Come on. We've got to hurry!"

Nancy took a second to calm herself, then made herself continue in her crablike crouch along the roof. Another ten feet and she followed Joe in a leap to the roof of the next car. Joe turned around to make sure she was with him.

"Nancy—" Joe began.

Nancy saw a look of pure horror pass over his face as Joe glanced over her shoulder.

"Joe," she asked. "What is it?"

Joe grabbed Nancy's arm and twisted her around. "Look!" he said urgently.

Nancy saw what had terrified Joe. Coming up—not three hundred yards away—was a tunnel. Frank, still chasing the guy, had his back to them and the tunnel. There was no way he could know about it.

"Frank!" Nancy and Joe shouted in unison, but the wind carried their voices behind them. Frank heard nothing.

Nancy turned around again. They were nearing the tunnel. She and Joe could duck and would be safe, but Frank wouldn't know.

"We've got to warn him somehow!" Joe said desperately. "Frank!" he shouted again.

It was no use. The wind and the roar of the train worked together to drown out their cries. Nancy watched Frank Hardy and clutched Joe's hand, terrified for Frank.

"Frank!" she and Joe screamed together at the top of their lungs. "Duck!"

Then Joe pulled Nancy down flat against the roof of the train. A second later the darkness of the tunnel surrounded her.

Chapter

Five

FRANK HARDY swore he could hear his brother speak his name. He took his eyes off the guy in front of him for a split second to turn to look for Joe.

He almost came in direct contact with a solid wall of concrete and stone.

Frank fell to the roof, and the train's low whistle sounded in his ears as it shot through the tunnel.

His heart thudding in his chest, Frank tried to calm himself by taking several deep breaths. Too close, he thought. That one was too close.

When the train came out on the other side of the tunnel, Frank drew in a lungful of fresh evening air. It was almost a full minute before his muscles would obey him enough so he could pull himself up to look around.

Not ten feet in front of him, the guy he'd been chasing was trying to stand up again. He had ducked in time, too, Frank realized.

There was no time to waste now, though. Frank crawled the distance at top speed and shot out an arm for the guy's left foot.

"Hold it right there," he said through gritted teeth.

The guy kicked his right foot back, catching Frank on the jaw. Frank saw stars but managed to tighten his grip on the man's left ankle. The short man dragged himself forward, pulling Frank with him.

Frank reached up and threw his arms around the guy's waist, but with a violent heave the bearded man managed to pull himself free. He was standing, and Frank was kneeling on the metal roof now.

Before Frank could react, the guy whipped around and lunged at Frank with all his might.

"Hey!" Frank yelled as he realized the guy was trying to push him off the train!

Frank fought back by butting his head into the guy's stomach. But the blow had no effect. Frank's opponent kept pushing. Frank felt his knees sliding closer and closer to the edge of the train.

The man gave Frank one final shove, and Frank felt his legs slide over the edge. Even when the guy let go, Frank continued to fall.

Frank clawed desperately at the metal roof, but his fingers only slid on the cold steel. As his body was flying into the air, Frank made contact with a thin lip of metal, which he clung to with only his fingertips.

Pain shot through his arms as he tried to pull himself back onto the train. The gale-force wind created by the speed of the train ripped at him, doing its best to tear him loose.

Frank rested a moment, concentrating only on catching his breath and not letting go. Then he tried again to pull himself up.

It was no use. He was going to fall!

"Frank!"

In the dark Frank could just make out his brother's face peering at him over the top of the train.

"Joe!" he gasped. "I can't hold on any longer!"

"We'll pull you up, Frank," Nancy called.

Frank felt Joe grip his wrists and heard Joe order Nancy to anchor him.

Frank held his breath, trying not to think about what would happen if Joe's hands slipped.

"Use your legs, Frank," Joe told him.

Frank wedged his toes against the side of the

train. He couldn't get any traction until his shoes hit on a rubber ledge along a window. Frank pushed with his feet as Joe hoisted him up.

Joe dragged Frank halfway onto the roof as Frank used his legs to push himself the rest of the way on.

"That was . . . a close one," he panted.

"I thought I was supposed to be the stupid, risk-taking Hardy," Joe said, his voice harsh with relief.

Frank grinned. "Don't worry, I'm sure you'll do something dumber very soon." He checked out the roof in both directions. The guy they had been chasing was gone.

"He got away," Joe confirmed. "Nancy and I saw him go down the side of the train just after he pushed you. He took another ladder."

"Jack and Laurie should know about this," Nancy said. "That guy seems to have something against them. Or this trip."

"Or both," Joe offered. "Come on. Let's see if we can find him inside the train."

Two hours later Nancy, Frank, Bess, and Joe had thoroughly searched the train. The man they were after was nowhere to be found, and no one had seen him.

"How did he get on in the first place?" Jack wanted to know. They were standing in the hallway outside Jack and Laurie's compartment. The Lerners were clearly shaken by the recent events.

"And who is he?" Nancy added. "Why would he be so intent on ruining this trip?"

Laurie grimaced. "He must be a crackpot," she said. "What other explanation is there?"

Frank shrugged and looked at Nancy. Who he was was the question that was on both their minds. "Unless we find him, we'll never know," he said.

"Let's just hope he doesn't strike again," Jack said, tugging at his tie to loosen it. "Laurie and I have put a lot into making this trip a success. Not to mention Brigston's investment. We can't afford to have anything go wrong."

"You're sure you didn't recognize the man back at Union Station?" Nancy asked.

"Was there anything familiar about him?" Joe put in.

"He could have been a customer at Jimmy's," Jack offered, "but his face didn't ring a bell—no."

"We've searched the train," Frank said, "and come up empty. I don't think there's anything more we can do tonight."

"Thanks again for all your help," Laurie said, looping her arm through Jack's. "I realize all this is taking time away from your solving our mystery."

"That's okay," Nancy said with a laugh. "Tomorrow we'll be in Emerald and get a chance to do some solid investigation."

They said good night to Jack and Laurie, then headed for their own compartments. Bess turned in the narrow corridor to study Frank. "I don't know how you can be so calm after what just happened to you," she remarked.

"Me, neither," Frank agreed. "Maybe I know that if I think about it too much, I'll realize just how close I came—"

"Don't think about it, then," Nancy said, cutting him off. They were at her compartment now, and she unlocked her door. "Think about the Comstock Diamond instead."

Bess beamed. "And the reward, Frank. Don't forget the reward!"

"Frank! Bess! Hurry up!" Nancy shouted. She was standing in the station parking lot in Lincoln, Nebraska. A bus was waiting to take them all to Emerald, the town on Ralph Machlin's map.

The morning sun warmed Nancy through her blue cotton sweater and white jeans.

"What's taking them so long?" Joe asked. "Frank's usually the first one ready," he said to Kate, who was standing with them.

Kate smiled and adjusted the paisley scarf that held her long red curls in place. "And guys are always saying girls take forever," she said.

Nancy laughed. She'd taken an instant liking to Kate, who was friendly and outgoing. Paul Fox, on the other hand, spent most of his time with the Lerners, or alone—much to Bess's despair.

Finally Frank and Bess stepped off the train and hurried toward the waiting bus.

"I had to go back for my guide," Bess explained, donning a neon pink baseball cap that was the exact same shade as her sneakers. An orange top and cropped green pants completed the effect. Nancy knew they were the "in" hot colors, but she wasn't convinced they should all be worn together. "Frank waited for me while I looked for it," Bess added.

"I've been reading my fact sheets," Bess announced as she took the seat next to Nancy. "Jake Comstock lived in Emerald for a while before he headed west."

Frank sat across the aisle from them, and Joe and Kate sat together behind him.

"Maybe the thief was trying to find a Comstock relative in Emerald?" Nancy said. "Maybe he hoped to demand some sort of ransom for the diamond."

"You mean he might have tried to sell it to some relative of Jake's?" Frank asked.

48

Nancy smiled at Frank's dubious expression. "Sounds pretty farfetched, I guess," she admitted.

"Maybe he hid it here, though," Bess offered.

"Maybe," Nancy told her friend, "but we still don't know why the thief was following Jake's route in the first place."

"*If* he was," a voice said, interrupting them. Connie Everett turned around in the seat in front of theirs to face them. "I still say that hack Machlin has us on a wild-goose chase."

"What makes you think that, Mr. Everett?" Nancy asked.

"Call me Connie." Everett knelt and leaned over his seat back. "Who are you kids?"

Nancy introduced herself, Bess, and Frank. "That's Joe, Frank's brother, talking to Kate Harkins."

Everett nodded. "Anyway, about Machlin. The guy was a big talker—if he was on to something, you can bet he would have boasted about it to me. But he never said word one. Nah, I'll bet you he just made this stuff up to sell a book."

Nancy wondered if Everett was just upset that Machlin hadn't told him about the Comstock research. "Did Machlin need money?" she asked out loud.

"He always needed dough," Everett said.

"His books weren't selling, and he was having a hard time getting publishers to look at his stuff." He shook his head. "Don't get the wrong impression—the guy was my buddy—but I wouldn't let my sympathies get in the way, if you get my drift. Mysteries are about facts, not feelings."

Nancy felt the bus pull to a stop. Jack stood up at the front and spoke to the group. "This is Emerald. By now most of you have some idea of what to look for. Let's all meet back here"—he checked his watch—"at two o'clock. And good luck."

As people stood up, Nancy bent down and stared out the window. Downtown Emerald was small—a dusty main street with a dozen low buildings strung along it. "Where do we start?" she asked Frank.

"Let's get any background information we can," Frank said. "We don't know what we're looking for, so we shouldn't narrow what we're going to research too much."

After they got off the bus, the group began to split up. Maggie Horne went off with John Gryson. Lee Goldstein came over and shook Everett's hand.

"Connie!" he said. "We haven't had a chance to talk yet. How've ya been?"

Everett returned Goldstein's shake. "Good, Lee. So tell me—what's your angle?"

Goldstein pulled on Everett's arm in a conspiratorial way. "Well, the way I see it, it's like this . . ." he began, leading Connie away from Nancy, Frank, and Bess.

"Kate and I are going to poke around the town," Joe said. "We'll get more done if we split up," he added weakly.

"Sure, Joe," said Frank, glancing in Nancy's direction. Nancy smiled and shrugged.

After Joe and Kate had left, Nancy, Frank, and Bess stood on the sidewalk, deciding what to do. The sun was beating down, and it was unusually hot for a fall day.

Bess coughed and rubbed her eyes. "I need a soda before we do anything. The dust and heat are making me thirsty."

Nancy looked at her watch and let out a sigh. It was past eleven, and they hadn't done a single bit of investigating.

"It's okay, Nancy," Frank said, sensing her frustration. "Just because all these other guys are off with their notes and their cameras doesn't mean they're on the right track."

Bess led them across the street to a coffee shop.

Once inside, Bess ordered a soda and a tuna fish sandwich. "It is almost lunchtime, after all," she explained.

"Where are you all from?" their waitress inquired. The name tag on her pink uniform read "Sharon." "I've lived in this town my whole life, I've been working in this here coffee shop for twenty years, and I know about everyone in this town. I haven't seen you three before," she added without taking a breath.

"We came from near Chicago," Bess announced.

"We're looking for information about a guy named Comstock," Nancy added. It was worth mentioning—if Sharon had lived in this town all her life, she might know something about Jake. "He was a miner and spent a couple of months here way back during the Gold Rush."

"Ever heard of him?" Frank asked hopefully.

"Now, isn't that funny," said Sharon, setting three glasses of water in front of them and shaking her head in disbelief.

"Isn't what funny?" Frank asked.

Sharon leaned on the counter and spoke to them confidentially. "Fifteen years ago a guy came into this coffee shop asking the very same questions you're asking now!"

Chapter

Six

"Aʀᴇ ʏᴏᴜ sᴜʀᴇ?" Nancy asked Sharon, barely containing her excitement. It was hard to believe they had stumbled onto a clue. If Sharon was right, they might have proof that the thief had been in Emerald. Still, she wanted to be sure.

"Fifteen years is a long time," Frank pointed out, exchanging a look with Nancy.

Bess beamed from under her neon pink cap. "I'll bet Sharon has a good memory," she said.

"You're right, I do," Sharon told her. "I even remember what dress I was wearing when I first met my husband."

"Sharon! Order's up!" the cook shouted from the end of the counter.

After Sharon left them, Nancy turned to Frank and Bess. "What do you think?" she asked.

"This is a small town," Frank pointed out. "If the thief really did stop here, chances are he'd end up in this coffee shop eventually. And Sharon's been here for twenty years."

Sharon came back with Bess's sandwich and a grilled cheese for Nancy. After she'd set them down, she put her elbows on the counter and rested her chin in her hands. "What's so special about Jake Comstock, anyway?" she asked.

Nancy swallowed a bite of her grilled cheese. "We're not sure. The guy you say was asking questions about him stole a diamond that once belonged to Jake, we think. In fact, he passed through here right after the theft."

"But why?" Sharon asked.

"He may have been looking for a Comstock relative to sell the diamond to," Frank suggested.

Sharon answered a call and went to refill a cup of coffee for a customer at the far end of the counter. "Well," she said after she had returned, "I'll tell you what I told him. There haven't been any Comstocks in Emerald in a hundred years. I don't even reckon Jake stayed that long."

The elderly man whose cup Sharon had refilled cleared his throat. "Sharon's right," he said. "I know because my great-great-uncle on my father's side went west with Jake."

"And he didn't leave any family behind?" Nancy asked. "Mr.—?"

"Kyle Hobbes," the man said, standing up to walk over and shake Nancy's hand. "And the answer is no, he didn't have any family."

"Why else would the thief want information about Jake Comstock?" Bess wondered aloud.

"Maybe he wanted to figure out where Jake went from here," he suggested. "Why I don't know."

Nancy reached over to grab Frank's arm. "That's it!" she cried. She turned to Kyle. "Do you know where they went?" she asked eagerly.

"Same place most prospectors went," Kyle told them. "Central City, Colorado."

"And that's the next stop on our map." Bess pointed to a dot she had circled in the middle of the Colorado Rockies on her map.

Frank raised his eyebrows. "So far, Ralph Machlin's research is holding up," he commented.

Nancy folded her napkin and placed it beside her half-eaten sandwich. "Well, I guess we can stop wondering about whether we're on the right track or not," she said. "That leaves us with only one question."

"Only one?" Frank looked impressed.

Nancy blew out a long breath. "How in the world are we going to solve this case?"

Joe and Kate had followed Emerald's main street out of town until it turned into a narrow road. They were walking along it now, and Joe was trying to find the right moment to ask the actress about Paul Fox.

"I'm sorry about last night," Kate apologized.

Joe was confused. "About what?"

Kate looked down at her flat black shoes. Joe noticed they were covered with dirt. Maybe he should suggest they turn back.

"Oh, you know," Kate said, looking up at him with her penetrating green eyes. "When Paul came along, I felt you got the wrong impression."

"What impression is that?" Joe asked gently, hoping it wasn't obvious what was on his mind.

"That we're involved or something." Kate sighed. "I mean, we were—involved, that is—until a few weeks ago, when we got into a big fight."

"Do you want to talk about it?" Joe asked. He tried not to sound eager to hear the details.

Kate bent over, picked up a stone, and tossed it at a distant tree. She hit it.

They walked in silence for a few minutes, and then Kate began to speak. "One afternoon when we were working at the Lerners' restaurant, I took a call for Paul from his agent. It was for a final audition for a good part. I left him a note about it, but he never got it. He's sore because he didn't make it to the callback, and he thought he'd get the part for sure. But the lost note wasn't my fault," she insisted.

"He's still furious?" Joe guessed.

Kate nodded. "He won't talk about it, and we don't see each other anymore, but sometimes he still acts like we're going together."

"It must be hard for you to have to see him," Joe said.

"It is." Kate smiled sadly and kept walking. "Paul and I still work together at Jack and Laurie's. I'd stop, but I need the money and Laurie's been so good to me. She even gave me this pin." Kate showed Joe the brooch at her throat. It was silver, set with a large blue stone, and looked like an antique.

"It's very nice," Joe acknowledged.

Kate went on. "It was even nicer of her to

ask me on this trip. Paul and I aren't really working, except for a couple of songs and a couple of scenes we're supposed to act on the last night. Laurie just asked us along to help *us* out. She knew that Paul and I needed a ride to get to Hollywood. We're going to be auditioning for Mike Isaacs—he's a hot agent out there, so she offered us this ride. It was really nice of her."

"Are you worried about the audition?" Joe asked.

"*Worried* isn't the word for it," Kate said. "Isaacs doesn't take many people. We were lucky even to get to audition for him."

Joe checked his watch. It was nearly two. "We should be heading back," he said. "Maybe tonight you can have dinner with me and my brother?"

Kate smiled. "I'd love to. Sorry I missed breakfast. I'm not a morning person."

During the trip back to Lincoln, Frank briefed Joe on what they had learned in Emerald.

"So we're on the right track," Joe concluded when Frank had finished.

Frank nodded. "But Nancy and I still wonder *why* the thief was following Jake Comstock's old trail."

Joe thought about it for a minute. "It is weird, isn't it? I wonder what the rest of the group found out," he said, glancing around him.

Maggie Horne was writing in a notebook. She glanced up to see Joe looking at her and quickly covered her pad with a book.

"It doesn't look like she's going to tell us, does it?" he asked his brother.

Frank shrugged. "Don't forget there's a reward at stake. Most of these people could use the money."

Joe kept his mouth shut and smothered a laugh. Some people might need the money, but not Maggie Horne. She had written several best-selling mystery novels. No, Joe decided, Maggie Horne isn't worried about the reward. She just wants to win.

As they reboarded the train in Lincoln, Kate found Joe and gave him a peck on the cheek and thanked him for their walk. "I'm going back to my compartment to rest. See you at dinner?"

Joe nodded and stared after her with a goofy grin on his face. Frank elbowed his brother in the arm.

Joe felt himself blushing. "She's really nice, Frank. Don't you think so?" Joe looked over and caught Frank winking at Nancy and Bess.

"Come on, guys," Joe said to his friends. "Give me a break."

Nancy shouldered her purse. "I don't know what you're talking about, Joe," she said with a big smile. "What do you say we head for the lounge and get a soda?"

"Great idea," Bess said.

Jack and Laurie appeared in the lounge, counting heads and making sure everyone had boarded. They told the group they'd be resting in their compartment until dinner if anyone needed them.

All the guests were quietly discussing what they'd learned. Connie Everett and Lee Goldstein were poring over a map at a corner table.

After they had all downed two sodas apiece, Bess was reading aloud from her travel guide. Joe wasn't paying attention because he was focused on Paul Fox, who had just come into the car.

Bess looked up. "Paul!" she cried out. "Come over and sit with us. We were just—"

Paul interrupted without looking at her, his eyes fixed on Joe. "Have any of you seen Kate?"

"Did you try her compartment?" Joe offered. "She said she was going to rest before dinner."

"She's not there now," Paul said.

"Do you want us to help you look for her?" Frank asked.

"I've looked everywhere for her, and she's gone," Paul said, still staring at Joe with a challenging look. "What did you do to her?"

Chapter

Seven

WHAT DO YOU MEAN?" Joe demanded. He half rose from his chair, his blue eyes furious.

Frank pulled him down again. "Easy," he murmured.

Around them the other guests looked up from what they were doing. Connie Everett leaned back in his chair, nudged Lee Goldstein, and whispered something to him. Both men fixed their eyes on Paul, waiting to see what would happen next.

"If this is your idea of a joke, I don't think it's very funny," Frank said to Paul.

"No joke. Kate is not on this train," Paul replied tensely.

Connie Everett and Lee Goldstein stood up and headed over to them.

"Is there a problem?" Everett asked.

Nancy answered, "Paul seems to think Kate Harkins has disappeared." At Everett's astonished look Nancy went on. "He's searched the train and can't find her."

"Did you get a conductor to open her compartment?" Frank put in. "Maybe she's sleeping and didn't hear you knock."

"Well, I—" The actor seemed taken aback.

"Did you try the observation deck at the back of the train?" Joe interrupted next. "She likes fresh air."

Paul scowled. "I guess I'm not as up on her habits as you are," he muttered.

"I'm going to check on her," Joe said firmly. Nancy didn't miss the scornful look he gave Paul. "You coming, Frank?"

"Let's split up," said Nancy. "You guys try the observation deck and check around the forward cars of the train. Bess and I will get a conductor to open Kate's compartment."

Frank and Joe left, and Nancy was about to take off with Bess when Goldstein turned to Paul. "So, young man. What makes you think your friend is in trouble?"

"Let's just say I know it," Paul said ominously.

Nancy's breath caught in her throat when

she heard the tone in the actor's voice. "Is there something you're not telling us?" she said.

Paul didn't answer her question. Instead he said, "I'll come with you to her compartment."

Nancy led Bess and Paul toward the back of the lounge car.

"She's not in her compartment," Paul said as they swayed through the train. "I know she isn't. But we can check anyway."

"Why are you so sure?" Nancy stopped to ask.

Paul leaned his hand against a locked compartment door to steady himself. "Kate is temperamental. I've seen her pull this kind of disappearing act before."

"What do you mean?" Bess asked.

"I mean not showing up at rehearsals. She even missed a performance once," Paul said, running his hands through his blond hair. "Sometimes she acts first and thinks about the consequences later."

"Are you saying you think she got off the train?" Nancy asked.

Paul nodded. "I know it sounds crazy, but Kate does strange things."

They got to the conductors' lounge, a small, curtained-off room at the end of one of the sleeper cars. Nancy poked her head through the maroon plush curtains. A woman conductor sat inside, reading a newspaper.

"I hate to bother you," Nancy said apologetically, "but we need to open up a friend's compartment. We're sure she's in there, but she doesn't answer when we knock. We're afraid she may have fainted or something."

The woman got to her feet. "A fainter, hmm? Why do things always go wrong during *my* break?" She grumbled but smiled. "Sure I'll help," she added. "Let me get my key ring."

With the conductor in the lead, Nancy, Bess, and Paul made their way back to Kate's compartment. It was in the last car, along with Paul's and the Lerners'. At Kate's door the conductor pulled out her keys with a flourish. She unlocked the door and threw it open.

The compartment was neat as a pin, but Kate wasn't there. Nancy walked in and checked out the room. A book lay open on the pull-down table.

"I told you she wasn't here," Paul said.

Nancy stepped closer, and Paul and Bess crowded in behind her. There was a cup of coffee on the table, too, and an apple. The apple had one bite taken out of it. The flesh inside was brown, as if the apple had been sitting there for a while. Gingerly Nancy dipped a finger in the coffee. She grimaced. It was cold.

For the first time Nancy felt a prickle of alarm. Obviously Kate hadn't planned on leaving the compartment.

Nancy turned to meet Paul's gaze. "I think we should tell Jack and Laurie about this," she said quietly. "It looks as if you're right, Paul. Kate is missing."

"What are they talking about?" Frank sounded frustrated. It was after dinner, and the whole group was assembled in the dining car. Joe was talking to two men at the far end of the car.

Nancy sighed. Twice they'd gone through the train looking for Kate. They'd asked every passenger and conductor about the actress, but no one had seen her.

Finally Jack and Laurie were forced to call an unscheduled halt in Holdrege, Nebraska. Hank Jervis, a detective with the Holdrege police force, had boarded the train and conducted his own search. That, too, had come up empty. Now he was putting together a missing persons report.

With him was Greg Ashby, a detective on the Chicago police force who had been invited on the trip. The two of them had been talking to Joe for almost twenty minutes.

At last Joe headed back to their table. He threw himself into a chair and put his head down on the table on his folded arms. "I think Ashby believes *I* had something to do with her disappearance," he said.

Nancy patted his shoulder. "That's ridiculous," she said firmly. "We all know it."

Joe gave her a tired smile. "Thanks. But that and fifty cents won't even get me a soda."

"What do *you* think happened to her?" Frank asked his brother.

Joe hesitated. "I think she's somewhere on the train," he said at last. "Her stuff's still in her compartment. And she's got an audition with an agent in California," he added. "This trip was her way of getting out there for free."

He didn't mention the alternative that Nancy knew had gone through all their minds: What if Kate had met with some sort of accident? Nancy thought back to the safety chain that had snapped on the first night of the trip. Was someone out to get Kate?

And had that someone succeeded?

Just then the two detectives walked by their table with the Lerners.

"We'll send a report to the Lincoln police," Jervis was saying. "They'll keep an eye out for her. I'm sure she'll turn up in a day or two."

"I hope you're right." Laurie looked worried. "I can't understand why she'd take off like this."

Ashby cast a dark look at Joe. Joe scowled back at him.

"I'll be going now," Jervis drawled, putting on his Stetson hat. "If you think of something you haven't told me, you talk to Ashby here, and he'll contact me."

Jervis left the dining car. Laurie stood by Nancy and the Hardys' table, gazing after him. "I'll never forgive myself for this," she said to Jack. "What if they don't find her?"

"They will," Nancy heard Jack say.

Jack put his arm around Laurie and steered her through the car. When the other guests saw them leave, they all started getting up. Most of them didn't say a word as they passed Nancy's table. Only Connie Everett offered some reassurance.

"Don't worry, kids," he said, patting Joe on the back. "It'll all work out."

Lee Goldstein gave them a small smile and followed Everett.

Once the dining car was empty, Nancy started talking to her friends. "The way I see it," she told them, "we've got two mysteries here. What happened to Kate, and what's the connection between Jake Comstock and the theft of the diamond?"

Frank cleared his throat. "Actually, there's a third. Who's the guy who threw that punch at Jack and set the fire in the kitchen?"

Joe sat up, looking suddenly more energetic. "Right. So let's divide it up."

"Exactly what I was thinking," Nancy said. She looked at her reflection in the dark train window. "Frank, why don't you and Joe handle Kate's disappearance and work out the sabotage angle? Who was that bearded, short guy and why did he set the fire? Bess and I will keep working on Jake Comstock."

"Sounds good," said Frank.

Nancy stretched. "Bess, let's head back to our compartment. We need to go over everything we know about Jake Comstock and the theft."

"Right," said Bess, picking up her cap. "I want to read up on Central City, too. Especially now that we know the thief probably went there."

"See you tomorrow at breakfast?" Nancy asked Frank and Joe.

"You bet," said Frank. Joe was quiet. Nancy could tell he was really worried about Kate. As she and Bess left the dining car, she hoped that Kate really was still on board.

But if she was, Nancy thought uneasily, why couldn't they find her?

* * *

The next morning Nancy got up before Bess. After showering and putting on a pair of dark cotton pants and her favorite plum-colored mock turtleneck, Nancy left a note for her friend and headed for the dining car. Along the way she glanced out the window. They were almost in the Rockies now. Nancy spied snow-covered peaks in the distance.

With time to kill before breakfast, Nancy decided to head for the observation deck. She'd be able to get a better view of the mountains from there.

Nancy climbed the short flight of steps that led up to the small observation area. Just as she got to the top, the train came crashing to a stop.

"What on earth—?" she asked out loud. There was a couple holding hands and staring out the window. They turned to look at Nancy and shrugged.

"Some kind of signal trouble, maybe?" the man volunteered.

Nancy stared out toward the front of the train. They were stopped in a steep mountain canyon. Sheer walls of light brown rock rose on both sides of the train.

Up ahead Nancy saw the glint of metal. The heavy, insistent blast of their train's whistle made Nancy realize, with a shock, what was happening.

A train was coming down the canyon in their direction. Only it was headed dead for them—on the same track.

Chapter

Eight

NANCY RACED toward the flight of stairs that led down to the lounge car. The young couple gave her a questioning look.

"What's going on?" the man wanted to know.

The woman he was with stood up. "Is everything okay?" she asked.

"I hope so," Nancy said. She didn't stop to explain. Instead, she raced down the steps and into the dining car.

"Frank! Joe!" she called out, running over to the table where they were sitting with Bess.

"What's wrong, Nan?" Bess asked, her eyes opened wide.

Nancy took a deep breath to calm herself. "I think there's a train heading for us. On the same track," she added for emphasis.

"What!" Joe jumped out of his seat and pressed his face against the window. "You're right!" he shouted. "We've got to do something."

"Like what?" Bess demanded, growing pale.

"Get everyone off the train, first of all," Frank said. "Excuse me," he said in a loud voice. "I don't want anyone to panic, but there's a good possibility we're in danger. I think we should evacuate the train. Now."

All the passengers in the dining car stopped eating to stare at Frank. "That's quite a statement, young man," Maggie Horne said, adjusting her half-glasses. "Are you and your friends having a bit of fun?"

"I'm listening to the kid, Maggie," Connie Everett said, standing up. "The train's stopped, and the whistle's blowing like crazy. I'm not going to stick around to see if he's right or not."

With that Everett stalked out of the car. Maggie Horne whispered something to John Gryson. Gryson shook his head, then took her arm and escorted her out of the car.

Everyone else quickly followed. Nancy felt the train lurch backward, then stand still again. "Come on," she said to her friends. "We've got to get out of here ourselves."

A conductor and porter were standing at the end of the lounge car, getting everyone off the train. "Keep calm," they were saying over and over. "Everything's going to be all right."

Nancy rushed past them and jumped down from the train, with Frank, Joe, and Bess right behind. She stood by the side of the train and looked up ahead. Even though the engineer of their train kept blowing the whistle in short, frantic blasts, the train barreling toward them hadn't slowed down one bit.

Nancy studied the area. The train was in a narrow canyon with no place for the passengers to hide and protect themselves from a crash.

"I'm going up there," she said firmly, pointing to the engine. "There must be something I can do."

"Nancy, that's crazy!" Bess cried. "You'll get killed."

Nancy ignored her friend and started racing toward the front of the train. She didn't know what she could do, but she knew she couldn't just stand by and watch the trains collide.

Nancy spotted the redheaded engineer frantically pulling on the whistle. Nancy climbed the metal ladder that ran up the car and got into the engine room.

When the engineer spotted her, he rubbed the sweat out of his eyes and shouted, "Get out of here! Can't you see we're going to crash?"

He went back to pulling on the whistle with one hand and trying to get the train in motion with the other. "Why won't this move?" he cried helplessly. He was pushing hard at a lever in front of him. It wouldn't budge.

Nancy dashed over to him, trying to keep her eyes averted from the oncoming train. It was growing larger by the second and didn't appear to be slowing down. "Which way is it supposed to move?" she asked, grabbing the lever.

The engineer grunted, "To the left. But it's jammed."

Nancy reached over to help him move the lever. She pushed with all her strength, but it wouldn't budge.

The trainman gave her a desperate look. "It's no use," he said. "We've got to get out of here."

Nancy jumped off the side of the train, the engineer landing with a grunt next to her. They watched, mesmerized, as the oncoming train drew closer and became larger and larger.

When it seemed too late, Nancy heard the train's brakes squeal. The other train was trying to stop! But was there enough time and space to avoid a crash?

Nancy's heart beat wildly in her chest as she watched the train shudder and try to stop. Its brakes squealed over the sound of its own whistle. She held her breath as the metal giant continued to pound toward them.

Then, miraculously, twenty feet from where they were standing, the other train wheezed to a screeching halt. Nancy let out the breath she'd been unconsciously holding. The red-headed engineer stared down at her in disbelief. "That's about as close as they come," he said quietly.

Frank and Joe appeared at Nancy's side, with Bess not far behind. "What the—" Frank began, seeing how close the two trains had come to crashing.

The engineer from the other train had hopped out of the engine and was coming toward them. "Gary!" he said, recognizing their engineer. "Are you nuts? Didn't you see the signal back there?"

Gary stiffened. "It was green all the way, Ted, honest. Then the emergency brake kicked in, and I couldn't get the monster to start again to back her up. The gears got jammed."

Ted hoisted himself up into the engine. Gary

followed with Nancy and the Hardys right behind them.

"See?" Gary said, pointing to the lever he and Nancy had tried to move. "It's completely stuck."

Ted tried but couldn't budge it. "Something must be wrong with the electrical coupling system," he concluded. "That's the only thing that could make the controls jam like this. But that system is practically fail-safe! I can't imagine what could have gone wrong."

Nancy looked at Frank and Joe. They were all thinking the same thing—the mystery man they'd chased over the train roof might have been responsible for this, too.

"What would someone have to do to make the controls jam like that?" Frank asked Gary.

Gary lifted his cap and rubbed his forehead. Then he combed his red hair back with his fingers and pulled his cap on. "Well, I guess you might try to unfasten one of the links or cut the connecting cables that run the electricity between the cars," he said, scratching his beard.

"Cut a connecting cable? Wouldn't that release the car from the rest of the train?" Joe wanted to know.

Ted shook his head. "The only way to do that is from underneath the train. Couldn't be done without a special tool."

"I'll tell you one thing," Gary said. "If I find out that someone messed with this system, I'll have his head. He nearly killed us all."

Gary and Ted tried to get the lever unjammed. "We're going to have to do a complete search of all the connectors once we see if we can get this baby running again," Gary told Ted. "Looks like we'll be here awhile."

"Come on, guys," Nancy said, leading the Hardys down the ladder out of the engine. "Let's see if we can figure out what happened."

Nancy watched the conductor help the passengers back inside. "Let's check the connectors," she suggested.

"What connectors?" Bess asked, joining them. The color still hadn't returned to her face.

Nancy explained what Gary had said about cutting the cables that ran between the cars.

"So he thinks someone tried to do that?" Bess asked.

"It's the only explanation we have for how the controls got jammed," Nancy explained. "I guess if someone messes with the electrical cables that run between the cars, the controls go haywire."

"Wow," said Bess. "Do you think it was the same guy who set that fire in the kitchen?"

Nancy bit her lip. "Could be," she said.

"That means he's still on the train," Bess

concluded, looking worried. "We should tell Jack and Laurie."

"Why don't you do that, Bess," Nancy said. "Frank, Joe, and I can go through the train, checking the connectors."

Bess nodded. "I'll meet you in the dining car later," she said, taking off at a trot for the rear of the train.

Nancy stepped over to the baggage car that was right behind the engine and pulled herself up and inside. Once Frank and Joe were standing next to her, Nancy leaned over and lifted the metal plate that served as a walkway between the two cars. Underneath there were several cables snaking their way under the train.

"Which one carries the electricity?" Frank asked.

Joe shrugged. "I thought you were the one who's done all the research on trains."

Frank leaned over and fingered a cable. "I have, but they don't give you wiring diagrams. But I know what to do," he said, standing up. "We don't really need to know which one is the electrical cable."

"We don't?" Joe asked.

"Nope. All we need to do is look for any cable that's loose or has been cut. Gary can tell us if it's the right one."

"Good thinking," Nancy said, brightening. "I don't see any loose ones here. Do you?"

Frank peered down at the jumble of wires. "No. Let's check the next car."

One by one Nancy, Frank, and Joe checked all the cables connecting the cars. After a while, though, Nancy began to doubt they'd find anything. They'd gotten all the way to the last car and had struck out so far.

"Maybe Gary and Ted were wrong," she said, leaning over to pull up the metal plate. They were between the sleeper car where Jack and Laurie had their compartment and the one where theirs were.

"It's— Hold on," said Frank, examining the cables. He was quiet for a moment. Then he leaned closer.

"What is it?" Joe wanted to know. He bent down next to Frank.

Frank looked up at Nancy. "Check it out, Nan," he said.

Nancy leaned over. Her eyes followed one of the thick cables to a set of huge bolts that jutted out at the end of the car. All the other cables they'd checked had been securely bolted in place. But not this one.

When Nancy's eyes reached the end of the cable, she saw that one of the ends had been unbolted and was hanging loose.

Their saboteur had struck again!

Chapter

Nine

W HAT DO YOU THINK the person was trying to do?" Joe asked. "Strand the last cars?"

"Ted said you can't unfasten a car that way," Nancy reminded him. "The only way to do it is from underneath."

"Yes, but the saboteur might not know that," Frank pointed out. He stood up and brushed his hands on his jeans. "We should get Gary back here to fix this."

"While you guys do that, I'm going to find Jack and Laurie," Nancy said firmly. "Obviously the saboteur is still on the train."

"You're right, Nancy," Joe said. "This connector didn't come loose on its own. That guy is determined to stop this trip."

"Yes, but why?" Nancy pondered out loud. "Does he have something against Jack and Laurie personally? I mean, this stunt may have been an attempt to strand their car. Maybe he's trying to get rid of them." She frowned, steepling her fingers. "Or maybe—"

"Wait a minute," Frank said with a laugh. "I thought Joe and I were handling the sabotage angle."

"We are," Joe said firmly. "After we get Gary back here, we're going to search this train to see if we can't find some sign of the guy. We'll search for Kate again, too, while we're looking."

Nancy was glad to see that Joe was still optimistic about finding Kate. "Good luck." She checked her watch. It was already after eleven. "I doubt we'll be making it to Central City before noon—if they get the train running by then, that is. Are you guys getting off there?"

"That depends on whether we've finished searching the train," Frank said. "What do you think, Joe?"

Joe ran his hands through his blond hair and sighed. "I doubt we'll be done. You go ahead with Bess. Let us know what you find out."

Nancy nodded and headed off to the dining

car, her mind working overtime about what the saboteur's motives might be.

Maybe he was a rival restaurant owner from Chicago, Nancy theorized, hoping to put Jack and Laurie out of business by ruining the trip and their reputations along with it.

Then another thought occurred to her. What if the guy was attempting to find the Comstock Diamond, too, and simply wanted to delay the train? Maybe he didn't mean to harm anyone at all. So far, no one had gotten hurt. The fire had been minor. In fact, if the two trains hadn't ended up on the same track just now, all that would have happened when the saboteur unfastened the connector was that the train would have stalled. And the crossed signals that put both trains on the same track could have been an accident, pure and simple.

There were some holes in the theory, Nancy knew, but it was possible. She'd have to run her idea past Frank and Joe and see what they thought. In the meantime she'd ask Jack Lerner if he had any business rivals—any who were capable of sabotage. Then she'd really zero in on the Comstock theft.

In the dining car the group was discussing the near accident in hushed tones. Sara Finney was conferring with Jack and Laurie at a table in the corner.

Bess and Paul Fox were sitting together,

talking. Though Paul looked as discontented as ever, Bess's face was rosy and her eyes were gleaming. Nancy could tell her friend was basking in the actor's attention.

Nancy waved hello to Bess and headed over to where Jack and Laurie were sitting with Sara Finney. When she got closer to their table, Nancy heard Sara trying to persuade Jack and Laurie to cancel the trip.

"Brigston's can't afford to keep risking people's lives," she was saying. She played nervously with the bow of the multicolored scarf she wore around her neck.

"I understand your concern, Sara, but I'm telling you—these are freak incidents," Jack insisted. "At least give us one more chance."

Sara stood up from the table. "All right. We'll keep going for now. But if anything else happens that endangers anyone, we're canceling the stops and heading straight through to San Francisco. Agreed?"

Laurie nodded silently and Jack gave Sara a thin smile. "Agreed. Thanks, Sara."

Sara took a deep breath and pushed a stray blond hair behind her ear. "I just hope I don't regret this. Brigston's will have my head if anyone gets hurt." With that she buttoned the jacket of her navy suit and strode away.

"Oh, Jack, we can't stop the trip now,"

Laurie said in a low, intense voice. Then she noticed Nancy standing beside their table.

"Nancy," she said. "Did you want to see us about something?"

Nancy took the seat Sara had just vacated. "Umm—I couldn't help overhearing you just now. I think we need to talk about all the incidents that have been occurring. I don't think they're accidents," she said gently. She hated to bring more bad news—Jack and Laurie already seemed really upset. But they had to know what she and the Hardys had discovered.

Jack rested his elbows on the table. "I checked with Gary, our engineer, and he's fairly certain the signal mix-up was an accident, pure and simple," he said defensively.

At Nancy's questioning look, he went on. "The track that leads to Central City is old, and it's not used that often. We got special permission to use the rail because it's the only way to get to Central City from Denver."

Laurie picked up from Jack. "Apparently, because the track isn't used that often, there was a signal failure. That's how we ended up on the track at the same time as the other train."

Nancy thought for a moment. "If the track isn't used that often, why was the other train on it?" she asked.

Jack shrugged. "That train has been touring mining sites on the old mining train routes. This area has quite a lot of them."

Nancy nodded thoughtfully. It looked as if she was right about the saboteur not trying to harm anyone. That should be welcome news to Jack and Laurie.

Still, the unbolted cable was no accident. She had a feeling that, once the news of it got out, Sara Finney wouldn't be willing to allow the trip to continue.

Sighing, Nancy explained to the Lerners what she, Frank, and Joe had discovered. "It's possible that these incidents are all being directed against you," she concluded bluntly. "Can you think of anyone who'd want to hurt you or ruin your reputation?"

Jack and Laurie exchanged a look. Laurie looked as if she was about to say something, but Jack spoke up quickly. "I really can't think of anyone, Nancy," he told her.

"You're sure?" Nancy pressed.

"I'll keep thinking about it, but right now I've got a more pressing problem on my mind," Jack said. "If you're right about all this, that saboteur is still aboard the train. We've got to find him before he strikes again!"

"That's what Frank and Joe are doing right

now," Nancy confirmed. "I suppose we should get Greg Ashby in on the search, too."

"We'll take care of that," Jack said.

Nancy felt the train jerk forward. "I guess Gary must have fixed the train," she concluded. "What happened to the other train?"

"They backed it up to the nearest junction and are waiting for us to pull through before they continue on to Denver," Jack informed her, glancing out the window.

"How long before we get to Central City?" Nancy wanted to know.

Laurie looked at her watch. "I think we should be there in less than half an hour."

Nancy stood up. "I'll go get ready," she told the party organizers. "But please think about what I asked you."

"I will, Nancy," Jack said with a smile. "Believe me, if I come up with the name of an enemy, you'll be the first to know."

"How about me?" Laurie asked with a laugh. "Don't you think I should know who it is, too?"

Jack laughed and leaned over to give his wife a hug. Nancy left them, glad to see that they were able to keep up their spirits even with all they were going through.

Before Nancy could reach Bess's table, her friend came toward her, a pained expression on her face. "Paul and I were getting along so well, Nancy, that I asked him if he wanted to tour Central City with us. He instantly got cold and unfriendly and said no, he'd rather stay on the train," Bess said. "What did I do wrong?"

Nancy put a reassuring arm around her friend. "Nothing, probably." Nancy didn't see any point in telling Bess that Paul Fox seemed like a jerk to her. "Forget about it. We'll have fun by ourselves."

Bess bit on her lip. "Okay, I'll cheer up, I promise. I just wish I knew what I did.

"Hey, do we have time to change?" she added, glancing down at her miniskirt. "Since Paul's not coming, I'd feel more comfortable in jeans."

"Sure," Nancy said, leading the way out of the dining car. "Laurie says we've got half an hour or so."

Nancy and Bess were just letting themselves into their compartment when they heard angry voices. They seemed to be coming from Frank and Joe's room. Nancy and Bess ran next door to find Frank, Joe, and Greg Ashby. From the expressions on their faces, Nancy could tell something had happened.

"What's wrong?" she asked.

Frank handed her a note. "Read this," he said. "We just found it lying on a chair in our room, and a copy was slipped into Ashby's room."

Nancy took the note. She scanned it, and then her voice caught in her throat as she read it aloud.

" 'Joe Hardy. You were the last one to see her alive. Why don't you tell us where she is?' "

Chapter

Ten

FRANK ANGRILY TOOK a step forward. "Joe had nothing to do with Kate Harkins's disappearance!" he said emphatically to Ashby. "Are you going to believe an insinuation in an anonymous note? That's ridiculous! Why are you wasting your time?"

Nancy had rarely seen Frank lose his cool. "Frank," Joe said. He laid a calming hand on his brother's arm.

"Take it easy, son," Ashby drawled. "I'm not accusing your brother of anything at the moment. I'd just like to get his opinion on who might have left this note. I want to know what that person knows—and how."

One name came immediately to mind. Paul Fox. Nancy looked over at Joe. Would he tell Ashby about the actor?

Joe only shook his head. "No, I'm afraid I can't help you," he told Ashby.

"No ideas?" Ashby sounded skeptical.

Joe looked straight into the detective's eyes. "No, sir," he said blandly.

Ashby grunted. "Let me know if you think of anything," he said, giving Joe a long look. Then he turned on his heel and left the car.

As soon as he had gone, Nancy faced Joe. "Why didn't you tell him about Paul Fox? The guy clearly doesn't like you," she said. "Maybe he wanted to get you in trouble."

"Paul?" Bess cried. "He wouldn't do something like that!"

"He might or he might not," Joe responded. He looked thoughtful. "But I want to find that out for myself." He turned to Frank. "Come on, big brother. Let's get a move on—we've got a lot more train to search today."

An hour later Nancy and Bess were wandering with the rest of the group along the hilly streets of Central City. The old mining town had been turned into a town for tourists. Gift shops and restaurants lined the streets.

One low wooden building had a sign outside

announcing that it was a mining museum. "Learn About the Men Who Mined the West," a note in small lettering offered.

"Come on," Nancy said, pulling on Bess's arm. "Let's do some research." She pointed at the sign.

"You don't think we'd find anything in there about Jake Comstock, do you?" Bess asked.

"You never know. It's worth a shot. He did live here, remember," Nancy replied.

Maggie Horne, who was standing nearby consulting her notes, gave a loud snort. "Take my advice, girls," she told them. "Don't bother with all that Jake Comstock nonsense. It will get you nowhere. Who cares *why* the thief was following Comstock's trail? That's not important. What's important is what the thief did along the trail."

"You're probably right," Nancy told her politely. "All the same, I think we'll look around a little."

Maggie shrugged and moved off with John Gryson. "Amateurs," the girls heard her mutter.

Bess giggled. "She always looks like she's just bitten into a lemon," she commented.

"Bess!" scolded Nancy with a grin. "Be nice. Now, come on, let's check out this museum." She walked inside, squinting into the gloomy interior. The place was small—only a few rooms. Dusty dioramas showing miners at work ran along its low walls.

Bess trailed behind Nancy as she toured the tiny museum. Worn picks and shovels were mounted on stands, and a few cases also contained documents and sepia-colored photographs of weathered, unsmiling men.

Nancy and Bess were the only visitors there. "Maybe Maggie was right," Bess said, her expression anxious. "Maybe we should be concentrating more on the thief and less on old Jake."

"Maybe," Nancy replied. She shook her head in frustration. "I don't know. I just don't know."

In the last room the girls found a tall young man standing at a cash register behind a counter. "Can I help you?" he called out. "We've got some gold nuggets for sale here, if you're interested."

"Actually," Nancy began, "we're looking for information about a miner who lived in Central City during the time when everyone was prospecting for gold here."

The young man's blue eyes brightened. "Now, you've just happened to mention my favorite topic. If there's one thing I know, it's miners. Name's Rich Miller, by the way."

Nancy shook his hand. "Nancy Drew," she said. "This is my friend, Bess Marvin."

Rich's eyes scanned Bess approvingly. "Nice to have some visitors every once in a while. It gets lonely in here," he said.

"Are you the only one who works here?" Bess asked.

"Just me and my dad, but he isn't here today. Today I'm cashier, janitor, and curator, all rolled into one. This museum is ours," he said with pride. Then he turned back to Nancy. "Now, do you want information about a specific miner? What was the guy's name?" he asked, leaning on the counter.

"Comstock. Jake Comstock," said Nancy.

Rich pulled himself up. "Joltin' Jake Comstock?" he asked.

"Joltin'?" Bess giggled. "Cute nickname."

"Well, Joltin' Jake was one of Central City's legends," Rich told them. "He had the best luck of any miner I ever heard of. They say he couldn't take a step without tripping over a nugget."

Nancy couldn't believe their luck in finding Rich. She told him about the Mystery Train, and why they were interested in Jake Comstock.

When she mentioned the Comstock Diamond, Rich rubbed the bridge of his nose thoughtfully. "I heard something about the Comstock Diamond once," he said. "What was it?" He screwed up his mouth and thought for a minute. "Now I remember. Jake had this big uncut diamond—it was his good luck charm. He never had it cut and polished, even though he could have sold it and made himself some money. But then, I guess Jake didn't need to sell the diamond—he had the golden touch."

"That's funny," Nancy commented. "I wonder what made him decide to have the diamond cut and polished later on."

"Do you think that's important to the mystery?" Bess asked doubtfully.

Nancy shrugged. "Who knows? I'll remember it, though."

Rick snapped his fingers. "Hey, you know what? I think I have a daguerreotype of Jake Comstock in the other room. Want to see what he looked like?"

"We'd love to!" Nancy said enthusiastically. "Rich—you're a gold mine of information."

"Pun intended," Bess put in, laughing.

The girls followed Rich into the front room of the little museum. He led them over to a case filled with faded brown portrait photographs of miners. "That's Joltin' Jake, third from the left," he announced, pointing at the case.

Nancy and Bess gazed at the old photograph. It showed a fair-haired man with a long, thin nose and high cheekbones. He was dressed in what was probably his Sunday best, a dark suit with a wide-brimmed hat.

"He reminds me of someone," Bess commented after a minute. "I can't think who. I hate when that happens!"

"It'll come to you later," Nancy said to her friend. Bess looked at the photo again, but no ideas came to her.

"You know, Jake Comstock supposedly found a mother lode of gold," Rich said. "But he never mined it. Instead he just filed a claim, then picked up and moved on west."

"What's a lode?" Bess whispered to Nancy.

Rich overheard her and grinned. "A lode is a vein of gold in the ground, usually in a bank of quartz. Most of the miners in this area mined silver, or they panned the streams for gold dust and nuggets. Jake did that, too. That's how he got rich."

"Did anyone ever try to find Jake's mother lode?" Nancy asked curiously.

Rich shrugged. "A few people did, I guess. Trouble is, no one knew exactly where to look. We don't have any good records of the old claims. And even if we did, the claim still technically belongs to the Comstock family—if there are any of them left." He whistled. "I tell you, if I were a Comstock, I'd be out looking for that lode. With the price of gold today, that thing must be worth millions!"

"Really?" Nancy said thoughtfully. Jake Comstock was beginning to be a very complex problem, she thought.

"Wow," said Bess. "This is all so neat!"

"You know, every so often someone comes around here asking about Jake Comstock," Rich said slowly. "When I was a kid and cleaned up here after school, I remember someone asking about him."

Nancy felt a prickle of excitement. "How long ago was that?"

"Fifteen years about. Let's see, I'm twenty-five now, and I couldn't have been more than nine or ten at the time."

Nancy frowned. Fifteen years—the timing was right. "Do you remember what the guy looked like?"

Rich shook his head. "It was a long time ago. All I remember was that he asked a lot of questions about Jake, his claim, the diamond. I could tell he wasn't from around here, though."

"Thanks, Rich," Nancy said. "You've been a big help."

"Anytime. You sticking around?" he asked, looking pointedly at Bess.

"Unfortunately, no," Nancy said. "We're leaving today."

"Well, see you around," Rich said. "Come back any time. I'll still be here." He gave them a wide grin as they turned to leave.

Outside, Bess grabbed Nancy's arm. "Can you believe our luck?" she asked. "Meeting Rich and learning all that about Jake Comstock?"

Nancy nodded absently. She was thinking about what Rich had said about the guy who had asked questions about Comstock fifteen years earlier. He must have been the thief!

Turning to her right, Nancy spotted a sign advertising tours of an original silver mine. A small train made up of what Nancy recognized as the cars that used to haul miners stood by an open shaft.

"That looks like fun," Bess said. "Want to take a ride?" she asked Nancy.

Nancy checked her watch. They still had a little time. "Sure, why not?" she agreed. Bess steered her over to the tiny train.

It was about to start. After buying their tickets, Nancy and Bess stepped into the last available car, right behind the small engine that pulled the train.

"It's kind of like an amusement ride," Bess said, pulling a rod down over their laps. "Although I never did like the fun house," she added in a worried-sounding voice.

Old rafters brushed their heads as the train entered the shaft. Inside the engine car was a small speaker. Nancy heard the voice of the woman driving the train tell the group about the history of the mine as they went deeper into the shaft.

The passageway got smaller and steeper. "Imagine being a miner and making this trip every day," the woman said in an ominous tone. "You wouldn't see daylight for eight, sometimes ten hours."

Bess clutched Nancy's arm. "This is spooky," she whispered.

Nancy looked around. The rough walls glinted with tiny bits of silver, and the shaft above their heads was dusty and full of cobwebs. "Don't worry," she said. "I'm sure it's safe."

The train kept up its steep descent. "Why are we going faster?" Bess asked nervously.

Nancy shook her head, sensing what Bess was talking about. The train was gaining momentum. She leaned forward in the car and saw the driver drop the microphone to grab on to the brake. She pushed at it frantically. But it was no use. The train was hurtling faster and faster down into the shaft.

"Nancy?" Bess cried. "What's wrong?"

Nancy grabbed at the bar that lay across their lap and pulled it up.

"I don't know, Bess," she said tensely. "But I have a feeling we're about to crash!"

Chapter

Eleven

BEHIND NANCY AND BESS a passenger screamed. Nancy began working her way out of her car.

"Where are you going?" Bess cried.

"I'm not going to just sit here. I'm going to try to do something!" Nancy shouted back.

Nancy struggled to keep her balance as the train raced down the tracks. She reached out and grabbed on to the side of the engine car. Carefully she lifted first one leg, then the other over the edge. She fell into the car in a heap.

The engineer was still pushing at the brake. When she saw that Nancy was in the car beside her, she yelled, "Get back!"

Nancy squinted down the tracks. She couldn't see the end of the shaft. Yet she knew that if they kept moving as fast as they were, they'd reach the bottom soon enough. There was no time to waste.

The engineer grabbed Nancy's arm. "You can't stay here," she insisted. With one hand on the brake, and her eyes on the tracks in front of them, the woman stood up halfway and reached out to push Nancy back.

Just then the train whizzed under a low rafter. Nancy watched in horror as the beam struck the engineer in the head! The woman crumpled to the floor of the engine car, her hand falling away from the brake.

"Nancy!" Bess screamed, having seen what had happened.

Nancy grabbed on to the emergency brake and pulled with all the strength she could manage, but it didn't move an inch. All the passengers were screaming hysterically now.

Up ahead Nancy could just make out that the track divided in two. One went down into the mine. The other went off to the right—uphill. Going uphill was their only chance. It would slow them down without needing the brake. But how was she going to get them on the other track?

Her eyes scanned the control panel. There

were at least a dozen levers. Which ones do what? she wondered frantically.

There was a grunt, then a body settled into the seat beside Nancy. "What should I do?" she heard Bess's breathless voice ask.

"Hang on to the brake," Nancy told her friend quickly. "I have to see if I can get us up there." She pointed to the other track, which was now approaching fast.

Bess held the brake handle. Again Nancy searched the control panel. Finally she spotted a lever toward the bottom on the left-hand side.

Please be the right control, Nancy begged silently. She grabbed the lever and waited until they were just about even with the spot where the track they were on joined the other track.

Now! She pulled the handle hard to the right. With a jolt the train veered onto the branching track.

It worked! As the train started uphill, it gradually began to lose speed.

"All right! We did it!" Bess shouted.

Nancy reached over to grab on to the brake. She and Bess both pulled hard. Finally Nancy felt the brake snap backward in their grip. With a wheeze the train slammed to a halt.

"Let me out of here!" a woman in the last car was shrieking.

Bess smiled, pale but game. "I'll try to calm

her down," she promised, and climbed over the seat toward the rear of the train.

The engineer was coming to now. Gently Nancy helped her up onto the seat in the engine car.

"What happened?" the woman murmured, holding her hand to the top of her head, where a nasty bump was appearing. She looked around her and saw they had stopped. "Oh, no," she said, obviously remembering now. "The brake was stuck," she began.

"It's okay," Nancy told her. "Everything's fine now. Can you manage to get us out of here?"

The woman took a deep breath, touched her head for a second, and put her hand on the controls. "I think so." She pushed in a throttle and the train roared to life.

"We're lucky—this track leads us right out of the mine," she explained. "And it's uphill all the way. That's good. I wouldn't want to depend on that brake right now."

"Let me know if you feel dizzy or anything," Nancy told her.

The woman nodded and moved the train forward. Nancy climbed over the side of the engine car and back into her car. In a second Bess rejoined her there.

"You girls saved our lives!" the man behind them announced. Nancy recognized him and the woman with him as the couple who had been in the observation area on the mystery train that morning. Behind them the other passengers burst into applause.

Nancy gave Bess a hug. "You did great," she told her friend.

Bess pulled back, and Nancy saw there were tears in her eyes. "I was so afraid," she said. "But I couldn't just sit by."

In a few minutes the train emerged from the mine shaft and pulled into a small yard. The engineer jumped out and raced over to a shed.

A man appeared at the door of the shed, and Nancy saw the engineer waving her arms as she told him what had happened. The two of them ran over to the train as the passengers got off.

Nancy watched the guy kneel down and peer under the engine car. "Someone jammed the gears on the brake, Gina," he told the engineer.

The woman knelt down beside him and took in a sharp breath. "You're right, John."

Nancy looked at Bess and then stepped over to where John and Gina were kneeling beside the engine car. "Did I hear you say someone jammed the brake?" she asked.

Gina turned to John. "She's the one who saved us after I got knocked out," she explained.

John stood up and shook Nancy's hand. "Thanks, miss—"

"Nancy Drew. This is Bess Marvin," Nancy said. John shook Bess's hand. "That was quick thinking on your part," he told them.

"What about the brake?" Nancy wanted to know. "Any idea who could have jammed it?"

John thought for a moment. "I can't believe any of my engineers would do something sick like that," he replied. "But, come to think of it, there was a stranger hanging around by the trains this morning. Scruffy guy. I didn't like his looks, so I told him to get lost."

Nancy and Bess exchanged a look. "Not again!" Bess wailed.

Gina pulled a strand of white blond hair out of her eyes. "Do you know this guy?" she asked.

Nancy explained about the mystery tour and the trouble they'd been having aboard the train. She described their saboteur to John. "Does that sound like the guy?" she asked.

John nodded slowly. "He was short and stocky and had that kind of salt-and-pepper hair you're talking about," he confirmed.

"Did you notice where he went?" Nancy asked.

"No, I didn't," John said, shaking his head. "The phone rang inside. It was Gina calling, so we chatted for a bit."

Gina poked John in the ribs. "You chatted. I was just calling to say I'd be late for work. Now I kind of wish I'd taken the day off."

Nancy grinned. "I know what you mean!" she said with feeling.

Nancy and Bess said goodbye. They were heading out of the small train yard when the couple who had been sitting behind them during their ride through the shaft came over to them.

"Excuse me," the man said. "I caught some of your conversation back there. So our ride was sabotaged?" Nancy nodded. "Do you really think it's the same guy who's been giving us all that trouble on the mystery train?" he asked.

Nancy nodded. "We think it might be."

The woman shivered. "This is too creepy," she complained. "I wish we'd gone to Niagara Falls like everyone else."

"Niagara Falls?" Bess looked confused.

"Pardon me," the man said hastily. "I'm Kevin Hughes, and this is my wife, Julie. We're on our honeymoon."

"Congratulations," Nancy said. "Excuse me for saying so, but this trip seems like a strange thing to do for a honeymoon."

"You're telling us!" Julie said.

"I was invited to attend—I'm a psychologist with the Saint Louis police force," Kevin explained. "The trip happened to fall right after our wedding, and since we wanted to go to San Francisco, we thought a train ride would be a romantic way to get there."

"Instead, it's turned out to be a life-threatening adventure," Julie said with a grin. "Not that it's not exciting, of course."

"I didn't know the police used psychologists," Bess commented.

Kevin nodded. "It's the wave of the future in criminology. We work on character profiles of suspects—their methods of operation, that kind of thing. I'd love to talk to you about this train saboteur, as a matter of fact."

"Later," Julie put in firmly. "I need to go back to the train and lie down, Kevin. My legs feel like rubber bands after that mine car ride."

Nancy was intrigued. "I'd like to go over the case with you later, Kevin. How about before dinner?" she asked.

Kevin reached out and shook both Nancy's and Bess's hands. "Great. See you then. Are you heading back to the train soon?"

Nancy checked her watch. "We still have an hour. Bess?"

Bess scanned the street. "There are all those souvenir shops we haven't checked out yet."

Knowing that nothing could stop Bess when

she wanted to shop, Nancy turned to Kevin and Julie. "You go on ahead. We'll see you later."

Forty-five minutes later Nancy and Bess had finally reached the end of Central City's main street. Bess was laden down with bags, and even Nancy had bought a necklace made out of semiprecious stones.

"That's a neat story about the woman whose face is painted on the barroom floor at the Teller Opera House, isn't it?" Bess asked Nancy. "I can't wait to put the poster up in my room."

Nancy smiled and glanced down the street at the small station where their train was waiting. Was it her imagination, or was the train pulling out of the station? "Bess," she said slowly, keeping her eyes on the train.

"What is it, Nan?" Bess asked.

"Does it look like the train's moving?"

Bess followed Nancy's gaze toward the station. "It's hard to tell from here."

Nancy pulled her friend by the arm and started racing down the street toward the station. Around them, tourists stopped to stare.

Nancy and Bess were still more than fifty feet away from the station when Nancy saw that she was right.

The train was leaving without them!

Chapter

Twelve

THE TRAIN'S LEAVING without us!" Bess wailed, struggling valiantly to keep up with Nancy. "What are we going to do now?" she cried.

"We can try to catch it," Nancy urged her friend. "Come on!"

The train wasn't moving fast yet. "We'll have to jump on board!" she shouted to Bess over her shoulder.

Nancy raced up to the tiny station at the end of the street and watched the train as it moved past her, picking up speed. As the dining car passed by, Nancy saw that the doorway was open. The metal stairs that led to the car hadn't been taken up yet.

"We'll have to make a run for it," she told Bess. She dashed alongside the train with Bess racing after her.

As soon as she reached the dining car, Nancy grabbed the stair's metal railing with her left hand. She held on tight and managed to swing her feet onto the stairs.

With her left hand grasping the railing, Nancy held out her right to Bess. "Grab on— I'll pull you up!" she yelled.

Bess was running beside the train, but it was moving faster now, and she had a hard time keeping up. "I can't do it!" she cried.

"Drop your bags and jump!" Nancy shouted to her. "It's the only way!"

Bess kept running, reluctant to let go of her souvenirs. She threw her right hand out, and Nancy managed to grab hold of her wrist.

"Drop your bags!" Nancy ordered her again.

Her legs dragging, Bess finally let go of the bag of souvenirs she was holding in her left hand. She pulled her arm around and caught hold of Nancy's hand.

With all her strength, Nancy hoisted Bess up. Bess managed to get a footing on the metal stairs. They were aboard!

"My poster—my gold nugget bath sponge,"

Bess wailed, her eyes glued to the bag of souvenirs lying on the side of the tracks.

"You still have the jewelry," Nancy reminded her, pointing to the bag that was looped around Bess's right wrist.

Bess leaned against the wall and caught her breath. "I know, you're right, Nancy," she said. "We did make it."

Nancy smiled. "Come on," she said, making room on the stairs for Bess. "Let's find Frank and Joe. We need to tell them that the saboteur struck again."

Nancy pushed open the door to the car and let Bess go through. Soon they were in their compartment.

Bess threw her bag on her bed and settled down next to it. "I think I'll stay here while you find Frank and Joe, if that's all right," she said. "It's been quite a day."

Nancy grinned at her friend. "No problem. See you later?"

Nancy made her way through the sleeper car and knocked on the door to Frank and Joe's berth. No answer.

Nancy decided to tell Jack and Laurie that the saboteur had struck again. After all, his last attack wasn't harmless.

She walked back to the last sleeper car and knocked softly on the door of Jack and

111

Laurie's compartment. After a minute or two Laurie appeared at the door wearing an off-white blouse and a red skirt. Her hair was pulled back, accenting her high cheekbones.

"Nancy," she said, looking surprised. "Is there anything wrong?"

"Can I come in?" Nancy asked.

Laurie nodded and opened the door wider for Nancy to step inside. Jack and Laurie's compartment was deluxe, like Nancy and Bess's. The double bed was folded up, and Laurie had pulled down the table from the wall.

"I was just doing some work," Laurie said, going over to the table and straightening up the papers on it.

Nancy spotted a couple of maps taped to the wall above the table. The first was an ancient-looking contour map.

The second map was more familiar. It was just like the route maps that had been handed out to all the passengers—only this one was not a photocopy.

"Is that the original of Ralph Machlin's map, by any chance?" Nancy asked.

"As a matter of fact, it is."

"May I look at it?" Nancy asked.

Laurie detached it and handed it to Nancy. "It's a bit of a mess," she said apologetically.

112

It's got Ralph's scribbles all over it. We cleaned up the copies for you guys."

Nancy scanned the map and noticed some faint pencil marks. "Are these Machlin's notes in the margins?" she asked.

"That's right. I tried to make sense of them, but Ralph used his own brand of shorthand." She reached to take the map back from Nancy.

"I'd like to keep this, if you don't mind," Nancy said. "There might be some kind of clue here that would help."

Laurie bit her lower lip. "I don't know if that would be right, Nancy. It might give you an unfair advantage."

"Just for the night?" Nancy asked. "I'll return it first thing tomorrow morning. Besides," she added as Laurie looked doubtful, "anyone else on the trip could have asked to see the original."

"Well—" Laurie hesitated. "All right," she said at last.

"Thanks," Nancy said. She glanced down at the papers. Suddenly her eye caught the word *Comstock* printed in bold capitals on some sort of legal-looking document, something like a deed. "What is that?" Nancy asked, pointing at the document.

Laurie began stacking the papers on the table. "Just something I'm working on, on my own," she said with a smile. "Nothing to do with this case. I'm researching a book on the San Francisco Comstocks, actually."

"You're writing a book on the Comstock family?" Nancy was intrigued. "That's quite a coincidence." She gestured at the contour map on the wall. "Is that part of your research?"

"Yes—yes, it is," Laurie answered. She seemed taken aback. "Now, you still haven't told me why you wanted to talk to me," she reminded Nancy. She hugged the stack of papers to her chest.

As Nancy told Laurie about the accident in Central City, the mystery ride organizer's eyes grew bright with worry. "That means the saboteur is still with us," she said.

"Or following our route very closely," Nancy pointed out. "No one has spotted him on board. He may have a copy of the route map himself."

"I should tell Jack about this," Laurie said. She stowed her papers in a manila folder. "Thank you for letting me know about this," she told Nancy as they moved into the hallway.

"Don't worry," Nancy said, trying to reassure her. "We'll get to the bottom of it."

Laurie sighed. "I really hope you do," she said in a weary voice.

Down the corridor of the same car Joe Hardy emerged from an empty compartment.

With the help of a conductor, he and Frank had been searching the train for what felt like hours. They hadn't uncovered a single trace of either Kate or the saboteur.

They'd unlocked and searched every compartment that wasn't occupied. Each one was completely empty, with no sign or clue of anyone having been there since the trip began. The woman who was unlocking the cabins for him was getting tired. Frank was up front, going through the baggage car one last time.

"What's in there, Karen?" Joe asked, pointing to a door at the very end of the car.

"That's the handicapped suite," Karen explained. "The officer back in Nebraska looked in there. Believe me, no one else has been in there since we left Chicago."

"Would you mind opening it?" Joe asked, walking toward the suite.

Karen sighed. "I'm telling you, no one's been in there."

"Let me check," Joe pleaded. "You never know."

Karen stepped past Joe and unlocked the door. Once she had it open, she flicked on the lights. Joe edged past her and went inside.

The suite was empty. The beds were made up into seats and the curtains were drawn.

"Can we go now?" Karen wanted to know. She looked at her watch. "I'm on duty in ten minutes, and I'd like to have a cup of coffee before that."

"Just give me a minute," Joe said. He went over to the pulldown bed and snapped it open.

Unlike the pulldown beds in the other compartments, this one was at knee level. "That's so people in wheelchairs can get into it without climbing up," Karen explained.

Joe nodded as he gazed at the neatly made-up bed. It didn't look as if it had been slept in. He was about to close it when he decided to run his hands over the blanket.

May as well be thorough, he thought, patting down the blanket. You never know. . . .

His hands detected a round object. Joe pulled back the blanket and then the sheet beneath it. His excitement mounting, he ran his hand under the sheet until his fingers found the object he'd felt. He grabbed it and pulled it out from under the covers.

It was a pin. The very same pin he'd seen Kate Harkins wearing the day she'd disappeared!

Chapter

Thirteen

KATE WAS HERE! I'm telling you, she was here!" Joe shouted.

"You're kidding!" Karen exclaimed.

"Look at this." Joe held out the pin for Karen to see. "It's hers—she was wearing it the day we were in Lincoln. I thought you said this suite's been locked since we left Chicago."

Karen looked at the pin again. "That's right," she said. She squinted at it and shook her head. "So I guess the next question is, how did the pin get in here?"

"A very good question," Joe said, raising one finger. "Who else has a key to this suite?"

Karen wrinkled her nose and thought for a moment. "Conductors. Trainmen—or women," she said with a smile. "The engineer might, too."

"No one else?" Joe asked, fingering Kate's pin. "Not even Jack Lerner or Laurie Adams?"

"You mean those people who organized this trip?" Karen asked. Joe nodded. "Nope," Karen said. "Not unless Jimbo gave them a set, which I doubt." She checked her watch again. "And speaking of Jimbo, I have to check in with him now."

"Jimbo?" Joe asked.

Karen grinned. "He's the conductor. He runs a pretty tight ship. He told me to report to him by four. It's five after right now."

Joe pocketed Kate's pin and snapped the bunk shut. "Thanks for all your help, Karen," he said as she closed the door to the suite behind them.

"No problem," Karen said. "Let me know if you need anything else." She headed toward the front of the train.

Left alone, Joe surveyed the last few locked doors. Was Kate behind one of those doors? he wondered.

He spotted Paul Fox heading toward him down the narrow corridor. At the same moment Paul caught sight of Joe. "Still looking for her?" he asked, with a sarcastic lilt to his voice. "Any luck?"

Joe hesitated for a moment, trying to decide whether or not to tell Paul about finding Kate's pin. He didn't trust the actor. He was almost positive, in his own mind, that Paul Fox had left that anonymous note. The real question was, did Paul do it just because he disliked Joe, or did he do it because he knew what had really happened to Kate?

"No luck," Joe said finally.

"My guess is she's back in Chicago already," Paul said. "She never was reliable, that Kate."

"What makes you so sure she got off the train?" Joe asked, fingering Kate's pin in his pocket.

"She was a nervous wreck, man," Paul told him. "She probably told you how we're going to audition for Mike Isaacs," he added.

"She mentioned it, yes," Joe answered.

Paul shook his head slowly. "I think she couldn't take the pressure. She got so terrified that she just took off. Like that." He snapped his fingers to emphasize the point.

Joe doubted Paul's theory. From everything Kate had told him, Joe knew she was thrilled at the idea of auditioning for a Hollywood agent. She might have been nervous but not scared enough to take off.

"How about you?" Joe asked Paul. "Are you nervous?"

Paul showed his perfect white teeth in a fierce grin. "I'll make it," he said. "With or without Kate. I've got three monologues down cold, and I still have a few more days before the audition. No, there's no way I'm going to blow this chance!"

Joe thought the actor stood a good chance of being a star with his all-American looks and fierce determination. "Well, good luck," he said.

Paul pulled on Joe's arm. "Don't get me wrong," he said, scowling. "I want to find Kate. She deserves a chance, even if she did cut out and leave me without a scene partner."

"You bet she does," Joe said, turning his back on the actor. Paul Fox gave him the creeps. "Take it easy," he said over his shoulder as he left.

Joe headed for the lounge, wondering if Fox's competitive streak was strong enough to make him get rid of Kate—a possible rival. That's ridiculous, he told himself. Or was it?

In the lounge Joe spotted Frank, Bess, and Nancy seated at a table with a couple he didn't know. Through the window beyond them, he saw mist collecting around the Rockies. A cloud passed, and the late-afternoon sun peeked through, sending splashes of light across the aspen trees and reflecting brightly on the snow-covered peaks. It was an awesome sight.

"Meet Kevin and Julie Hughes," Nancy said as Joe sat down. "They're on their honeymoon."

Julie smiled. Kevin put out his hand to shake Joe's. "We were right behind Nancy when that little train almost crashed in the mine shaft back in Central City," he explained.

"Hold on," Joe said, looking at Nancy. "Back up. What happened?"

Joe listened as Nancy briefly related what had happened to her and Bess in Central City, including what Rich had told them about Jake Comstock and the diamond, and how Rich remembered a guy asking questions about Comstock fifteen years earlier. She ended with the news that the train had almost left without them.

"How could the conductor not know you weren't aboard?" Joe asked when she was finished.

"When we got back on board, we told that actor—what's his name?" Julie asked, turning to Kevin.

"Paul Fox," Kevin stated. "Jack and Laurie weren't around, but we ran into Paul and mentioned that you and Bess were still in

Central City. He said he'd tell Jack and Laurie so they wouldn't leave without you."

Bess drew in her breath sharply.

Joe scowled. "Paul Fox strikes again."

"Maybe he just forgot," Bess suggested. Nancy and Joe were very dubious.

"What do you mean, he 'strikes again'?" Kevin wanted to know.

Joe told them Paul's theory about why Kate left the train. "But look what I found." Joe pulled the pin from his pocket. "It's Kate's. She'd never have left it behind."

"So you think she never left the train, huh?" Frank asked his brother.

Joe nodded. "Right. And now I'm wondering if Paul Fox had something to do with it."

"Why?" Kevin asked, leaning his elbows on the table.

Joe leaned back in his chair and told them what Kate had said about the stiff competition to have Mike Isaacs for an agent. "He takes so few people on as clients that getting rid of Kate eliminates one person right away. And Paul *really* wants to be represented by him. Besides that, he had a grudge against Kate because he blamed her for not getting a message to him about a callback."

Frank rubbed his chin thoughtfully. "I think you're stretching it, Joe," he said.

"Maybe not," Kevin put in. "Joe's theory is psychologically fairly sound."

At Frank's questioning look, Julie proudly explained, "Kevin's a psychologist. He works with the Saint Louis police on developing character profiles."

"What do you think about Paul?" Frank asked Kevin.

"He's under stress. He already has a reason to want to hurt Kate, if Joe's right about this callback." Kevin paused and made circles on the table with his finger. "Maybe it is a bit of a stretch," he admitted after a moment. "We're talking about very extreme behavior. But it's possible that he saw Kate as an obstacle and decided he had to get her out of the way."

"By kidnapping her?" Nancy asked, keeping her voice low. "That seems like an awfully complicated way of stopping her from auditioning, doesn't it?"

"Yeah! Nancy's right," Bess said, her face brightening.

Nancy glanced at the lounge clock. "Why don't we discuss this over dinner?"

"Dinner?" Joe repeated. "It's only five o'clock!"

Frank stood up from the table. "Dinner is early tonight. Laurie announced it just before you came in. Paul's performing at seven, and after that they're showing *Murder on the Orient Express* in the lounge."

Joe grimaced. "Let's hope no one gets any ideas."

"Especially the saboteur," Bess said with a shiver.

"What do you think about what happened in Central City?" Joe asked Frank as they followed the rest of the group to the dining car. "Is the guy on the train, or is he following us?"

The Hardys took seats at a table with Nancy and Bess. Kevin and Julie had plans to eat with some of the other guests, so they went off to meet them at the other end of the dining car.

"We can't find any sign of him on board," Frank replied. "The only alternative is that he knows our route and is keeping up with us by car."

As Joe was sitting down, Connie Everett appeared at their table. "Heard about your accident," he said to Nancy. "Are you okay?"

"I'm fine, thanks," Nancy told him.

"You'd think the trip was cursed," Everett said, shaking his head.

Lee Goldstein came up to them. "Cursed? Connie, you sound like those B movies I used to write. Come on, let's eat."

Everett and Lee took the table next to Nancy and her friends. In a minute or two waiters came around to take their order cards. "Mmm, I have to say this train food is better than what I cook at home," Nancy heard Connie say. He smacked his lips and unfolded his napkin. Nancy suppressed a grin. She liked Connie— he was kind of crude, but funny. Underneath it all, she suspected, he was also a bit of a softie.

Just as they were finishing the main course, Greg Ashby passed by.

"I want to talk to you after dinner," he said, addressing Joe. "In my compartment." Without waiting for a reply, he strode off.

"Oh, boy," said Joe, looking after the man. "I get the feeling I'm about to be arrested."

"That can't happen," Nancy said. "He's got nothing on you. He's probably just looking for a lead. Hey, speaking of leads, I almost forgot!" she added, hitting her forehead with her hand. "When Bess and I got back, I stopped by Laurie's compartment. She lent me Ralph Machlin's original map. There are some penciled notes of his in the margins—I thought it might be worth looking over. Do you guys want to check it out?"

"I do!" said Bess. "I can't believe you forgot about that, Nancy. You're losing your touch," she chided.

From the next table Connie Everett cleared his throat. "I wouldn't mind having a peek at that map," he said, leaning over to address Nancy. "I might be able to decipher Machlin's chicken scratches."

"Good idea," Nancy agreed.

"All right if I stop by after the movie?" Connie suggested. Nancy nodded.

Joe stood up. "I'd better go see Ashby," he said. "I'll meet you guys later."

"Can you handle it alone?" Frank asked Joe. "I'd like to go over the map with Nancy."

Joe nodded. "Sure. I'll let you know what happens." He sighed.

He left the table. Nancy gazed after him, her eyes troubled. "I hope Ashby isn't too rough on him," she said to Frank.

"Joe's tough," he said. "Let's just hope he keeps calm."

Nancy knew what Frank meant. Joe could be hotheaded sometimes.

Laurie Adams and Jack Lerner hurried by their table. Nancy raised a hand in greeting, and Laurie gave her a harried smile. "We've got a million things to do. See you all later at the movie," she called.

They were walking back to Nancy and Bess's compartment when a thought that had been nagging at Nancy for a while finally surfaced. She snapped her fingers. "What if two of our cases are really one? What if the saboteur kidnapped Kate?" she suggested to Frank and Bess.

"Hey, that's a good thought," Frank said excitedly. "You mean, suppose Kate accidentally stumbled on the saboteur while he was fixing the electrical cable, or something, and he had to get her out of the way?"

"Right," Nancy agreed.

"Nancy!" Bess cried. "You're a genius. I take back what I said about you losing your touch. Of course that guy has her!"

Nancy was turning the key in her lock. "Not so fast," she cautioned. "We don't have any proof. And even if we are right, we still don't know where Kate is."

"But it's a good theory," Frank confirmed. "I'll go over that angle with Joe when he's finished with Ashby."

"Fine," Nancy said, reaching in to switch on the light. "Right now, though—"

She stopped dead, taking in the sight that greeted her.

The room was a shambles. Clothes were everywhere, and the luggage had all been pulled out of the closet.

"Oh, no!" Nancy cried, rushing over to the closet.

"What is it?" Bess asked. Then she gasped as she saw the mess in their compartment.

"My suitcase!" Nancy said, frantically searching for it. "I put the map in it to keep it safe, and—oh, thank goodness, my suitcase is still here!"

"Better check inside," advised Frank. He strode to Nancy's side.

"Good idea." Nancy popped the latches on her battered black suitcase and threw open the lid. Her shoulders drooped.

The suitcase was empty. The map was gone!

Chapter

Fourteen

"WHEW, THAT'S BIZARRE," Frank said. "Who would think to look there?"

"Yeah—who could have taken it?" Bess asked.

"That depends on who knew that Nancy had it," Frank said, standing back from the closet to survey the room. "Whoever it was was intent on finding it."

"As far as I know, you guys and Everett and Lee were the only ones who knew I had the map—other than Laurie, of course," said Nancy. "*She* wouldn't have stolen it—if she needed it back, all she had to do was ask me. It doesn't make any sense."

"Maybe Laurie let it slip to someone else," Bess suggested. "And maybe that person wanted to look at it before you did."

"Think for a minute," Frank said, clearing a space on the seat next to the window. "Did anyone see you with the map before you stashed it?"

Frank watched as Nancy stepped away from the closet and stood in the middle of the small compartment. She pulled back her reddish blond hair with both hands and held her head for a moment. "I came straight from Laurie's compartment. I don't think I passed anyone on the way." She paused. "Wait a minute—"

"What?" Frank and Bess asked in unison.

"While I was coming down the hall, I was looking at the map and I nearly bumped into Maggie Horne."

Frank met Nancy's eyes, and he let out a low whistle. "Did she notice that you had the map?" he asked.

"Yes, she did," Nancy said. "I remember now because she started asking me questions about Joe and Kate and the sabotage on the train, but the whole time she was looking at the map."

"Wow," said Bess. "Who would ever think that prim-looking lady is nothing more than a common thief!"

Frank held up his hands. "Hold on. We still

don't know that she is. Sure, she may have seen Nancy with the map, but that's no proof that she broke in here." He rested his hands on his knees and leaned back in the seat. "Although," he added, thinking aloud, "I'll bet she does know how to pick a lock."

"We can't just walk up to her and accuse her of stealing the map," Nancy said. Frank detected a hint of frustration in her voice. "Can we?"

"No way," Bess piped up. "She'll give you that steely look of hers, and you'll wither and die on the spot."

"Bess is right," Frank agreed. "Either we have to sneak into her compartment and look for it and run the risk of getting caught ourselves, or we wait it out and see if we can't trap her into a confession."

"I'm not too keen on the idea of breaking in," Nancy said. "If Maggie Horne catches us and she's innocent, we could be in big trouble."

Frank had to agree. "So we wait it out," he concluded. "We'll have to tell Laurie, though."

"I know," Nancy said with a sigh. "I'd like to put it off until morning, though. Who knows, maybe it'll turn up."

Frank raised a skeptical brow. Nancy sighed again. "Not likely, I know. Still, I'd rather wait. You know, I don't know which is worse

—having to tell Laurie the original is gone, or not being able to look it over."

"Look what over?" Joe asked, popping his head into the compartment.

Frank had been expecting his brother to be in a foul mood after his discussion with Ashby, but Joe seemed okay. He quickly explained to Joe about the missing map.

"Maggie Horne!" Joe exclaimed. "Who would have thought—"

"As I told Nancy and Bess," Frank said, "we don't have any proof. And I for one don't want to go around accusing the grande dame of mystery writers of being a thief."

Joe held his hands up as if protecting himself. "Me, either. I'll bet she bites!"

Nancy and Bess laughed. "How'd it go with Ashby?" Nancy asked. "You don't seem too upset."

Joe flopped down on a seat. "I'm not! Fact is, Ashby's off my case—that anonymous note seems to have convinced him that I'm innocent. He's a pretty sharp guy, actually. He realizes that whoever left him that note is much more likely to know something about what really happened to Kate. He wanted to see me because he wants my cooperation from now on."

"So he doesn't think you had anything to do with it?" Nancy asked.

"Nope," said Joe. He leaned forward, stretching the kinks out of his muscular frame.

Frank slapped his brother on the back. "That's great news!" he said.

Joe shrugged. "It would be even greater news if we could find Kate," he said.

"Any word from the police in Lincoln?" Frank asked.

When Joe shook his head, Frank asked him if he'd told Ashby about finding Kate's pin.

"I did," Joe said. "And he was pretty excited about it. He agrees with me that Kate's still on the train. The question is, where?"

Frank didn't miss the frustrated look that passed over his brother's face. "You want to keep looking for her, don't you?" he asked.

At Joe's silent nod, Frank thought for a moment. "I think you should."

"Not *us?*" Joe gazed quizzically at Frank.

"When the train stops in Kearns tomorrow, I think I should go with Nancy and Bess and the rest of the group," Frank announced.

"You do?" Nancy asked, surprised.

Frank explained his reason. "Last stop we made, the saboteur struck outside the train. I want to keep my eyes open for him, see if he does it again." Frank glanced at Joe, hoping his brother wouldn't mind being left alone. "We've been over this train twice now," he

133

said gently. "There's no point in both of us looking again."

Joe seemed to think about what Frank had said. Finally he turned to his brother. "You're right, Frank. You should go with Nancy and Bess. There aren't too many places left to look. I guess I can handle it."

"Thanks," said Frank, grateful that Joe understood. He checked his watch and looked around Nancy's compartment. "Now I think we should help these two straighten this place up. It's almost time for the movie."

The next morning after breakfast Nancy, Frank, Joe, and Bess were sitting on the observation deck. They were about an hour and a half away from their next destination—Kearns, Utah. Joe looked out the window over Nancy's shoulder at the retreating mountains in the distance.

"Look!" Nancy said, pointing behind Joe. "The Great Salt Lake!"

Joe turned in his seat. As the train came out of the mountains and headed toward Salt Lake City, they had a great view of the huge, saltwater lake. The ground around it was bare and brown, with hardly any vegetation at all.

"It's so barren—I feel like we're looking at a lunar landscape," Joe said in awe.

"Why are we stopping in Kearns?" Bess asked.

"It's the closest town to Copperton, where the copper mines are," Nancy told her. "From Kearns we take a short bus ride."

"What happened to Bess Marvin, tour guide?" Joe teased. "I thought you had all the answers."

"I have my guidebook right here, Joe Hardy," Bess retorted. "I was just testing Nancy."

The other three burst out laughing. "Oh, right!" Joe gasped.

The train passed through Salt Lake City and fifteen minutes later came to a halt at a small junction. Joe saw a sign from the train window that read "Kearns." The countryside had flattened out, but off in the distance to the left, across a vast plain of sagebrush, he could see a low mountain range with huge mounds dotting its foothills.

"Those must be the mines," Frank said, pointing.

"It says here this area is loaded with copper and silver mines," Bess said, reading from her guidebook.

"That's why Jake Comstock passed through, no doubt," Joe said, spotting a bus parked by the train. "You guys should get going. People are boarding the bus."

"Okay, we'll see you in a few hours," Nancy told him.

"Good luck," Joe called as the other three left the observation deck. "I hope you get a solid lead."

"Same to you," Frank said to his brother.

After they had left, Joe sat for a while on the observation deck. The area was empty. From the window he could see the bus pulling out of the parking lot. A moment later he spotted Paul Fox hurrying across the lot toward the train. He disappeared into the doorway of the last car.

So he's staying behind, is he? Joe said to himself. He decided that now was as good a time as any to confront Paul with his suspicions. If the actor had anything to do with Kate's disappearance, Joe wanted to know.

As Joe headed toward Paul's compartment, he passed by Jack and Laurie's suite.

I'll bet no one ever looked in *their* compartment for Kate, Joe suddenly thought. It was a crazy idea—he couldn't think of any reason why Jack and Laurie might be hiding Kate. But it was possible. . . .

The door was locked, but with a practiced twist of the smallest blade on his pocketknife, Joe unlocked the door and slipped inside. He switched on the lights and quickly looked around.

136

The compartment was a mess, with clothes and papers strewn all over the place. Joe pulled open the closet and several suitcases tumbled out, making an alarming racket as they fell. But there was no sign of Kate.

Well, that was that. Jack and Laurie didn't have anything to do with Kate's disappearance. Joe hadn't really thought they had.

Joe glanced at the pulldown table next to the window. On it were several untidy piles of papers. What caught his eye was the old, spidery script lettering that read "This Claim" all in capital letters. It was some sort of legal document, Joe realized.

"Neat," he said, picking it up. It was a sheet of paper clipped to an old, hand-drawn contour map of what looked like a section of the Rocky Mountains.

Then his eye happened to fall on the next sheet in the pile. What he saw made him stop in his tracks.

Unless he was wrong, Joe was looking at the very same map that had been stolen from Nancy's compartment the night before!

Chapter

Fifteen

JOE REACHED OUT and grabbed the map. It had to be the one Nancy lost—it looked exactly as she had described it, with pencil markings in the margins. He licked his finger and rubbed some of the ink. It ran.

That cinched it. The map was the original!

Now, how did this get from Nancy's suitcase to Jack and Laurie's compartment? Joe wondered.

Could Laurie have been the thief? Why steal back something that she could have asked for?

At that moment Joe heard footsteps in the hall. A second later came the dreaded sound of a key fumbling in the lock.

Joe's heart stood still. He made a dash for the closet door—maybe he could hide in there until whoever it was went away. But at the last minute he remembered all the suitcases inside. They'd fall out when he opened the door. The noise alone would advertise his presence.

It was no good. As Joe stood there helplessly, the door swung open. He found himself face-to-face with Jack Lerner.

"Uh—J-Jack," Joe stammered, meeting the man's stare. "I—" He paused, racking his brains to come up with an explanation for what he was doing in Jack's compartment.

Jack seemed utterly startled for a moment. Then his expression changed to anger. He glanced down at the door. "Was this open?" he asked.

Joe cast his eyes to the floor. "Actually, no," he said. He tried to think of a good way to get himself out of the jam he was in. Finally he decided to tell the truth. "I picked the lock," he admitted.

Jack crossed his arms and leaned against the doorway. "Want to tell me why?" he asked, icily polite.

"I was, well, I was thinking that all this time I've been looking for Kate, I never looked here." Joe hoped Jack wouldn't make the logical connection—that a part of him had suspected Jack and Laurie of being behind Kate's disappearance.

But from the expression on the mystery ride organizer's face, Joe realized he'd hoped in vain. "You think Laurie and I had something to do with Kate's disappearance?" Jack demanded. "That's absurd!"

Joe reached out a hand. "No. I mean—well, maybe I did. I guess I wasn't thinking straight."

"No, I don't think you were." Jack stepped past Joe and into the room.

"Look," Joe began, "I'm really sorry—"

"No, no." Jack held up a hand. "Breaking into our compartment was stupid, Joe. But I can see you're distraught about Kate." He paused. "I suppose that, under the circumstances, I understand."

"You do?" Joe asked, meeting the man's eyes in surprise.

Jack smiled. "I know what it's like to be young," he told Joe. "You do foolish things."

Joe swallowed his annoyance. He didn't think he was doing anything in the least bit foolish, but he doubted it would be a good idea to debate this point with a man whose compartment he'd just broken into.

Jack went on. "You really think finding that pin is proof that she's still on the train?"

At Joe's definitive nod Jack pursed his lips. "There are several places where she could have gotten off, you know," he said. "And we've searched high and low for her. I don't think she's here. You're wasting your time, Joe."

Joe was silent. He knew he couldn't give up, but there was no point in wasting time arguing about it. He was in a hurry to find Paul Fox and confront him with his suspicions. "Right. Well, I should get going," he said.

Jack saw the map in Joe's hand. "Were you planning on taking that?" he asked.

"Uh—no," Joe said, handing it over. "Do you mind if I ask you how it got here, though?"

Jack took the map from Joe. "I'm starting to feel defensive, Joe," he said, shaking his head slowly. "First you break in here because you think Laurie and I are holding Kate hostage, and then you imply I stole the map from Nancy."

Now Joe felt even more embarrassed. "Well, I—" he began. Then he realized it wasn't such an absurd idea. After all, the map did disappear from Nancy's suite, only to turn up in Jack and Laurie's compartment. "In a way, it's a logical conclusion," he told Jack.

"Karen found the map this morning, stuffed under our door," Jack explained. "I decided to keep it here for safekeeping. I planned to tell

Nancy that we'd located it, but the group had already left for Copperton."

"When I see her, I'll tell her you've got it," Joe suggested.

"Fine." Jack put the map on the table with the rest of the papers. "Now, if you don't mind, I have some work to do."

Joe nodded and went to the door. "Sure. Look, I really am sorry about everything. No hard feelings?"

Jack waved his hand absently. "No hard feelings. You know, I can't imagine why someone would steal this map. Do you think it was the same guy who's been giving us so much trouble?" he asked.

"Could be." Joe frowned. "But I doubt it. He doesn't need it. He seems to know our route. Besides, how could he know Nancy had it?"

Jack rubbed the back of his neck wearily. "You're right. One more mystery."

Joe opened the door, his mind already on his conversation with Paul Fox. "Don't worry," he said. "One way or another we'll have them all solved by San Francisco."

Frank stared out the bus window. Ahead of them to the south, low desert mountain ranges dotted the landscape. "What are your thoughts on the Comstock angle?" he asked Nancy, who was sitting next to him. "Any idea what we're looking for here?"

Nancy glanced past Frank and out the window. "Well, the place we're going to is a copper mine. I guess Jake did all kinds of mining. Anyway, this mine is near Copperton—an old mining town. Bess says it's the largest open pit copper mine in the country."

"That's the world, Nancy." Bess leaned over the aisle to correct what Nancy had said.

Sara Finney was sitting next to Bess. "You sure have done your research," she told Bess.

Bess turned to her. "You bet," she said, and immediately began reciting to the Brigston's representative all the facts she'd learned.

Frank nodded his head at Bess and grinned at Nancy. "There's one person Machlin's research isn't wasted on," he commented.

"Good old Bess. She does know her stuff, doesn't she?" Nancy said with an admiring laugh. Then her eyes turned thoughtful. "You know, I really wonder how Machlin uncovered all this information," she said. "I mean, how did he ever get the idea that the diamond thief was following the path of a forty-niner? And how did he figure out just what that path was?"

"I have a feeling that if we knew that, we'd be a lot closer to solving the mystery," Frank answered. "It's really too bad about that original map vanishing. I bet that between us and Connie Everett, we might have gotten a couple of leads from Machlin's scribbles."

Nancy groaned. "Don't remind me," she said.

"Sorry." Frank took out his copy of the map. "Okay, let's get to work. As I see it, we've got a break in the pattern coming up."

"Really?" Intrigued, Nancy took out a pen and paper from her shoulder bag. "Shoot."

"According to Machlin's research," Frank said, "Jake's next stop was Reno. That's not a mining town, is it?"

Nancy thought for a moment. "Not that I know of. It is in the middle of mining country, though. Besides, it was the largest town between Utah and California. He had to stop somewhere."

"Okay, maybe. But what about San Francisco?" Frank wanted to know.

Nancy tapped her pen against her cheek. "Well, that wasn't part of his trip west, exactly. Remember what Jack told us the first day? Jake settled in San Francisco and became a banker." She pulled out her information packet and consulted a piece of paper. "It says on this biography sheet that he used the money he'd made in mining to open the Comstock Bank and Trust."

"Oh, right," Frank said, deflated. "Smart

guy." He looked out the window again, letting his thoughts wander over the clues they had so far. He saw what looked like a small town up ahead. "That must be Copperton," he said to Nancy, pointing out the window.

"I guess so," she said. "Apparently we're heading for the mine first, but we'll stop in town on the way back to the train."

Frank put his hands behind his head. "Okay. Before we get to the mine, let's figure out what we're looking for," he said. He paused. "The thief was on Jake's trail. Why? If he just wanted to stash the diamond somewhere until the police stopped looking for it, he didn't have to do it in such a roundabout way."

"True," Nancy said. "Maybe he was looking for a particular place to stash it," she suggested, looking thoughtful. "Some place that only Jake knew about. Like one of his old claims."

"But why?" Frank wanted to know. "What would be the point?" He made a little gesture of frustration. "This whole mystery is so vague," he complained. "We're looking for a diamond that's been hidden for fifteen years, somewhere between Chicago and San Francisco—we *think!* Do you realize that's more than half the width of the United States? That's a lot of ground to cover. If only we had one concrete clue! Looking for one of Jake

Comstock's old claims," he muttered half to himself. "What good would that do anyone?"

Suddenly something Rich Miller had told her came back to Nancy. She laid a hand on Frank's arm. "Hey, remember I told you that Jake Comstock supposedly left an unmined claim somewhere?" she said in a low voice.

Frank looked puzzled. "I remember. What about it?" he asked.

"Well, if it really does contain that mother lode, as Rich Miller says, then it's worth a ton of money—a lot more than any diamond," Nancy explained. "Now, our mysterious thief seems to have known quite a bit about Jake Comstock. What I'm getting at is, suppose he heard the stories about the old claim? We do know he asked Rich about it."

"You mean, suppose his trips to these sites had nothing at all to do with the diamond? Suppose he was just trying to find the mother lode?" Frank groaned. "Nancy, you're bringing in a whole new mystery here. The old one is confusing enough already!"

"Sorry," Nancy said with a guilty grin.

"Besides," Frank went on, "I thought that unmined claim was somewhere around Central City."

Nancy shrugged. "Maybe the thief didn't know that," she suggested.

"Maybe," Frank echoed. He gave Nancy a sideways glance. "What do you want to do about it, then?"

"I don't know," Nancy was forced to admit.

A few minutes later the bus pulled to a stop. Laurie stood up at the front. "We're here!" she said brightly. "Meet back at the bus in two hours. Don't forget we stop in Copperton on the way back."

Frank followed Nancy and Bess out of the bus. Outside, the air was full of dust from the mine. There were huge mounds of dirt and a staircase leading from the ground level up to the top of one of the mounds.

As the group climbed the stairs, Frank let his thoughts wander on the mystery. What was the thief looking for? He had the diamond. All he had to do was hide it and wait to sell it. Why hadn't he done that? Why was he following Jake Comstock's path instead?

Frank slowly climbed the stairs behind Nancy and Bess. Suddenly he heard Bess give a cry of surprise. When he got to the top of the stairs, he understood her reaction.

In front of him a huge pit spread out in an irregular shape. It had to be at least two and a half miles wide and a mile and a half deep. He could barely make out the bulldozers and dump trucks that were working it.

"Impressive, isn't it?" Connie Everett said, standing beside Frank. "But I'll let you kids in on a little secret that's even more impressive."

Frank glanced at Nancy and Bess and exchanged a smile with them. "What's that, Connie?" he asked.

Everett paused. Then he poked a finger at Frank's chest and announced in a dramatic voice, "I've solved the mystery!"

Chapter

Sixteen

YOU MEAN you've found the diamond?" Nancy cried.

Everett's smug expression rapidly vanished. "Well—not exactly," he confessed.

"So what do you mean you've solved the mystery?" Frank asked him.

"I mean I know who took it," Everett said, keeping his voice low. He looked over his shoulder. Nancy saw Maggie Horne staring at them with icy blue eyes. "Look, can you keep this under your hats?" Everett asked them. "I don't want the whole world to know."

"If you don't want anyone else to know, why are you telling us?" Nancy asked.

"I want to know *what* he's telling us," Frank said firmly. "Did you solve the crime or not?"

Everett motioned them to a corner of the overlook. "I solved a huge chunk of it," he told them when they were standing away from the rest of the group. "And Goldstein wasn't one bit of help, I might add. That guy should stick to writing movies—he doesn't know the first thing about real crime. But I'd appreciate it if you didn't tell him I said that," Everett added.

"We won't," Nancy said. She tried to steer Everett back on track. "What exactly have you figured out?"

"I like you kids," Everett said. "I like your style. That brother of yours was in hot water, but he didn't let it get to him. I like that. So I'll tell you." He leaned in and looked at Nancy with his watery brown eyes. "It was no common thief who took that diamond. It was the Mastermind!"

"The Mastermind?" Frank echoed. "Who's he?"

Everett pulled back and stuffed his hands in his jacket pockets. "Only the most creative jewel thief of the past fifty years." He shook his head slowly. "I can't believe it. I've researched him and everything. All the facts were staring me right in the face, and I didn't put them together until we were on that bus. Goldstein and his little theories were distracting me, I guess."

"Exactly how does this guy operate?" Frank asked. "And what makes you so sure it was him?"

"Slow down, Frank," Nancy urged. "Why don't you take it one fact at a time?" she said to Everett.

"Right." Everett pulled his hands out of his pockets and counted his fingers. "Fact: The Mastermind specializes in hitting auction houses. The security generally isn't as tight as at a jeweler's. Fact: He's a pro, and Sara Finney said it was a professional job. But the most important fact of all is this crazy, out-of-the-way route he took for stashing the diamond."

"What do you mean?" Bess wanted to know. "We know he was following Jake Comstock."

Everett's laugh came out as a wheeze. He pulled a handkerchief out of his breast pocket and put it over his mouth. When he had finally stopped laughing, he said, "You kids kill me. You really do. You don't buy that whole Comstock line, do you?"

Nancy saw the color rise in Bess's cheeks. "But—" Bess began.

Nancy interrupted her friend. "You're saying Jake Comstock didn't have anything to do with the route the thief took?" she asked Everett.

Before Everett could answer, Frank broke in. "In both Emerald and Central City, people remember a guy coming around fifteen years ago, asking about Jake Comstock."

"It's a red herring, kids," Everett said. "You guys know what that is, right?"

Nancy nodded, but Bess looked blank. "A false clue," Nancy explained. She turned from Everett to look out at the mountains that surrounded them and thought for a moment. The dry desert wind blew through her hair.

"Let me see if I understand," Nancy said, looking back at Everett. "The thief pretends to be trying to find information about Comstock, but all the while he's just laying the groundwork for an elaborate wild-goose chase—just in case, fifteen years later, someone comes looking for him."

"That's crazy," Frank said. "No thief operates that way. He'd call so much attention to himself. Why not just disappear with the diamond?"

Everett threw his hands up in despair. "Okay, so I'm a crackpot. Is that what you're saying?"

Nancy was quiet. Secretly she didn't think Everett was taking the Comstock connection seriously enough, but she didn't want to say that to him. Besides, what if he was right?

"The Mastermind loves to leave false trails," Everett ventured. "He likes confusing the police. He likes to pop up, make himself obvious, then disappear. It's more fun for him that way. Maybe he almost wants to get caught," he added. "But no one has ever caught him. He's that good. Tell you the truth, I kind of admire the guy."

"So where do you think he actually stashed the gem?" Frank asked after a moment.

Everett sighed. "If I knew that, do you think I'd be standing here?" he asked with a shrug.

"Do you think he hid it along his route, or did he keep it with him the whole time?"

"You mean the diamond could have been in San Francisco all this time?" Bess asked, her eyes growing wide.

"I wouldn't be at all surprised," Everett answered. "Not one teeny bit."

Joe Hardy was definitely feeling frustrated. He was eager to confront Paul Fox and get his suspicions out in the open. However, the actor was nowhere to be found. Joe had knocked at his compartment door, and then looked for him in the lounge car. Now he was back at Paul's compartment, but Paul still wasn't there.

Joe made his way through Paul's sleeper car. His mind went to the map he'd found in Jack and Laurie's compartment.

It had to have been taken from Nancy's suitcase by somebody on the train. How did he—or she—know where to find it? And why did he—or she—return it to Jack and Laurie?

The Comstock Diamond case was getting very complicated, Joe mused. Maybe he should be spending his time on that rather than looking for Kate, he realized sadly.

Yes, it was time to move on. When Frank, Nancy, and Bess came back, Joe would really dig into the Comstock case. If Kate was gone, she was gone and that was that.

Joe reached out to the side of the car to balance himself just then. His hand knocked against the wall and made a hollow sound.

The noise caught his attention. Joe knocked on the wall again. It was definitely hollow.

His excitement mounting, Joe felt along the wall for a handle or hinges. He couldn't find a handle, but hidden underneath a little flap of metal he found a tiny hole.

Joe grabbed a ballpoint pen from his shirt pocket and jabbed the pen into the hole. The panel popped open, and Joe was staring at the inside of an electrical closet.

On the floor, with a gag over her mouth, was Kate Harkins!

Joe dropped to his knees beside her and pulled Kate into his arms.

It was the last thing he remembered. In the next second he felt a hard, dull thud at the back of his neck. A ringing blackness surrounded him, and he slumped to the floor.

Chapter

Seventeen

Do you think Connie Everett is right?" Bess asked Nancy as she put the finishing touches on a fresh coat of Imagine That Pink! nail polish.

Nancy and Bess were in their compartment, getting ready for the fancy dress dinner Jack and Laurie had arranged. Afterward, the ride's organizers wanted the group to share information on their progress on the mystery.

"If anyone knows about the Mastermind," Nancy told Bess, buttoning her black tuxedo pants, "I'd say it's Connie Everett."

"But does that mean it really is the Mastermind in this case?" Bess asked. She turned back to the mirror to smooth her royal blue flounced skirt over her hips.

Nancy tucked in her emerald green blouse and threw on an ivory dinner jacket. She shook her head. "I don't know. It's a good theory, and we'll have to follow it up."

"How are we going to do that?" Bess asked.

"When we get to Reno, we'll get any information we can about the Mastermind—like, where he was right after the theft." Nancy slipped on her black flats.

"Maybe the Reno police could find out from old FBI files, or something like that. I think Connie has a contact on the Reno police force, which is lucky for us."

Bess tilted her head and ran some gloss over her lips. "You know, I've been so caught up in this mystery that I haven't even thought about Paul. But tonight—"

Nancy touched Bess's shoulder lightly, her eyes twinkling. "That's the Bess I know and love. Are you ready?"

Bess checked that her nails were dry. Then she fluffed up her curls one last time and grabbed the royal blue purse that matched her dress. "Now I am," she said.

Nancy held the door open for her friend and switched off the lights.

"Hey, I almost forgot," Bess said as they headed off toward the dining car. "On the bus to Copperton, Sara Finney was telling me about the Comstock Diamond, and she says that Laurie Adams put in a silent bid on it when it was up for auction fifteen years ago. Pretty strange coincidence, isn't it?"

Nancy stopped dead in her tracks. "What! When were you planning on telling me this, Bess?" she asked.

Bess stuck out her lower lip just a bit. "I'm telling you now, aren't I? I would have told you on the bus, but you and Frank were so busy talking that I didn't want to interrupt."

"What else did Sara say?" Nancy prodded. "I thought she wasn't even working at Brigston's at the time."

"She wasn't," Bess confirmed. "She read through all the old files to get ready for the trip. There was a record of all the bids there. Do you really think it's important?" she added excitedly.

"I don't know. Laurie seems to be a lot more interested in the Comstock family than she's been letting on. She hasn't been doing any investigation on this trip, though," Nancy said, thinking aloud. "So even if she did bid for the diamond fifteen years ago, she doesn't seem to have a strong urge to be the one to find it now."

Bess shrugged. "Maybe that's why she was

so interested in Ralph Machlin's research—she already knew all about the diamond."

"That's probably true," Nancy said. "But why keep it a secret?"

"I don't know, Nan," Bess said. "Maybe she's just secretive by nature. Come on, we're going to be late."

Frank Hardy was already sitting at a table when Nancy and Bess walked into the dining car. His eyes were glued to the entrance to the car. When he spotted the girls, he raced over to them.

"Have either of you seen Joe?" he asked.

"No," Bess said, giving Frank a puzzled look. "Why?"

"Is something wrong?" Nancy asked, instantly alert. She thought she caught a note of extreme anxiety in Frank's voice.

Frank nervously ran a hand through his dark hair. "I don't know. Maybe. Maybe not. He isn't in our compartment. I've looked all over for him, but I can't find him."

Nancy's eyes opened wide. "You don't think—" she said softly.

"I don't know what to think," Frank said with exasperation. "Maybe he got off the train in Kearns and we left without him. Or maybe whatever happened to Kate has also happened to him."

159

"You think that's what's happened, don't you?" Nancy asked. "Why?"

"It's just a feeling," Frank answered, keeping his voice low as the other guests filtered into the dining car.

"Have you told anyone else?" Nancy queried.

"Yes." Frank nodded. "As soon as I realized Joe was gone, I found Greg Ashby. We went through the train looking for him. Not a trace."

Bess's soft blue eyes were distressed. "Wow," she breathed. "Poor Joe!"

"I talked to the conductor—he had a list of who was on the bus to Copperton. Everybody was on the list except Joe and Jack Lerner—and the train crew, of course," Frank told the girls.

Nancy studied his eyes. "But there's something else, isn't there?" she asked. "I can tell by your expression."

Frank gave a half smile. "As usual, you're right." He looked around the room to make sure they weren't overheard. "Paul Fox was signed up to go on the Copperton tour, but he didn't go—one of the trainmen saw him in the parking lot *after* the bus left. So it looks like he was around, too."

"Oh, say it's not Paul," Bess moaned. Her

eyes followed the good-looking actor as he moved from guest to guest, making conversation.

"It couldn't be Jack," Nancy said, frowning. "Could it?"

"I can't come up with any motive for him," Frank said, frowning. "He says he did talk to Joe for a few minutes in his compartment, but that was the only time he saw him."

"Have you spoken to Paul?" Bess asked.

"No—I haven't been able to get him alone," Frank replied, sounding frustrated. "And then there's always the possibility that our saboteur has struck again," he added. "But since there haven't been any more incidents aboard the train, I'm beginning to wonder if the guy's still with us."

The waiters had started serving dinner. "We should sit down," Bess urged.

Frank followed Nancy and Bess back to the table where he had been sitting. After they had sat down, Nancy leaned her elbows on the table. "What's the plan?"

Frank let out a long sigh. "Ashby said there isn't much we can do until we get to Reno. He did inform the police in Kearns, though."

Nancy and Bess were quiet as the waiter served them. There was nothing much to say, and during dinner they made only small talk.

Frank didn't even pretend to pay attention to the conversation.

"He'll turn up, Frank," Nancy finally said as the waiter cleared their plates. "I know he will. Joe's a resourceful guy—no one could keep him down for long."

Frank reached over to squeeze her hand. "Thanks," he said.

Jack Lerner stopped by their table on his way toward the front of the room. "I'm so sorry about your brother," he said to Frank. "But we'll find him, don't you worry." Then he turned to Nancy. "I wanted you to know that we found the map," he told Nancy.

"You did!" Bess said brightly. "That's great news!"

Nancy thanked Jack Lerner. "Any idea who might have taken it?" she asked.

"Jack!" Laurie called out across the dining car. "Let's get started!"

"No, no idea. Now, if you'll excuse me," Jack said. He walked across the dining car to where Laurie was standing. Soon he was rapping a spoon against his water glass and calling for the group's attention.

"It's been four days now since this trip started," Jack reminded the group. "We hope most of you have some solid leads by now. I'd like to open this session by asking if there's anyone who'd like to share what they know or pose a question to the group."

"I have a question," Maggie Horne announced. She stood up and cleared her throat. "It's occurred to several of us"—she looked down at John Gryson, who was sitting next to her—"that there's one possibility you and Laurie haven't taken into account. That is, what if we get to San Francisco, still haven't found the diamond, and don't realize until then that it's actually hidden in a spot we've passed?"

Laurie stood up. "Maggie has raised a very important point. In fact, I'm surprised no one has brought this up before now. Sara, would you like to answer that?"

Sara Finney spoke from her table. "Brigston's will investigate any and all leads that come from this trip. Jack and Laurie will see this through to the end, as well. Unfortunately, the reward applies only to whoever actually finds the diamond. You are all more than welcome to continue your search after the trip, too, in the hopes of getting the reward."

"Thank you," Maggie Horne said, sitting down again.

"Anyone else?" Jack asked the group. Frank watched as several people looked at their notes and conferred in small groups. Connie Everett and Lee Goldstein were sitting at a table next to them, having a heated discussion.

"Tell them," Goldstein was urging, holding on to Everett's arm.

Everett pulled back. "No way, Lee. This clue's mine. I don't want her"—he pointed his head at Maggie—"horning in on it. Ha-ha!"

Frank smiled at Nancy and Bess. "That guy's too much," he said.

Goldstein sighed and rolled his eyes. "Well, I'm going to tell them," he said, starting to stand up. "One of them might know what to make of that idea of yours."

"You'd better not!" Everett practically shouted, grabbing Goldstein's arm.

"Is there something wrong over there?" Jack asked Goldstein.

Goldstein yanked his arm away. "My good friend Connie Everett thinks this crime was committed by a famous criminal known as the Mastermind," he announced before Everett could stop him.

Everett sank in his chair and put his hands over his face.

"Connie," Jack said, "would you elaborate on what Lee just told us?"

Frank watched as Everett pulled his hands away from his face and stood up reluctantly.

Briefly he told the group what he had told Nancy, Frank, and Bess earlier.

When he was done, Everett sat down and turned to Goldstein. "I hope you're satisfied."

Goldstein looked smug. "I'll bet you ten bucks one of these people can take your idea and make something out of it. I've worked in Hollywood—collaboration is where it's at."

The noise of the crowd grew as they discussed the Mastermind, until a voice called out, "Before all you people get carried away, you should know the Mastermind was eliminated years ago as a suspect in this case."

Frank looked up and saw that Greg Ashby was standing now. The police detective held out his hands for silence. "Everett's idea is good. But the police have already investigated that angle. I was a rookie then, but I clearly remember that the Mastermind was ruled out."

Everett stood up and faced off with Ashby. "What makes you so sure it wasn't him, just because you ruled him out?" he demanded.

The crowd was hushed as the two men stared at each other. "Because he was committing a crime in Europe at the time!" Ashby announced.

Everett's face turned bright red. "B-but—" he stammered.

"So much for Connie's knowledge of the Mastermind," Nancy said. "It looks like we're back to square one."

The next morning the train stopped in Reno. Frank watched wearily as Nancy and Bess went off with Connie Everett. Joe still hadn't turned up, and Frank hadn't gotten much sleep the night before. He was feeling more than frustrated—where had Joe gotten to? He couldn't stand to consider the terrible possibilities.

Frank just hoped Nancy would have more luck. After Everett's theory about the Mastermind had been dashed at dinner, the rest of the evening had turned into a bit of a disaster. Everett had stalked out of the room, and the evening broke up soon after.

Now humbled, Everett had asked if he could help Nancy, Bess, and the Hardys with their investigation. Nancy was insistent on following through on the Comstock angle. She was convinced that knowing more about Jake Comstock was the only way to learn what the thief had been up to when he'd followed the miner's route. So she, Bess, and Everett were heading off to do research on Comstock in the hopes they might get a decent lead.

From the observation area, Frank spotted police cars pulling up to the train. True to his word, Ashby had enlisted the Reno authorities to help in the search for Joe and Kate. Frank was grateful for the Chicago detective's help. He watched as Ashby briefed the Reno police on the situation.

Then he noticed a short man with black hair shot through with gray, who was watching the scene intently. Frank's heart started beating in double time.

Unless he was very wrong, he had just spotted the saboteur!

"Hey!" Frank called out, jumping from the train.

The man saw Frank coming toward him and took off at a run. Frank raced after him, through the station and out onto the street.

Cars whizzed past, just missing them both as Frank chased the man across the street. The guy tore down the block.

"You're not getting away this time!" Frank shouted, putting on speed.

He chased the guy for two blocks, his longer legs allowing him to close the gap. Finally, on a deserted side street, he was near enough to make a flying tackle.

Frank threw himself on the guy, and the two of them tumbled to the sidewalk. Frank pinned the man's arms and sat on his legs. His opponent twisted and turned, but Frank held on.

"Forget it," he grunted. "This time you're caught!" Frank flipped the guy over so he could face him.

"Where is he?" Frank asked through clenched teeth. "What did you do with my brother?"

Chapter

Eighteen

THE MAN STARED BLANKLY at Frank. "I don't know what you're talking about," he said in a calm, almost polite voice.

Frank let go of the guy's arms and pulled back. Had he gotten it wrong?

In the second that Frank let go, the man sat up and knocked Frank off him, pulling his legs free. Off balance, Frank could only watch as the guy sprinted off.

Frank pulled himself up and took off after the guy, who was turning onto a busier street. He had a good head start, but Frank was determined not to let him get away this time.

On either side, neon lights advertising casinos and hotels blinked at Frank. Luckily, the sidewalks were not jammed, and Frank was able to keep his quarry in sight.

There was almost a whole block between them, though. Frank pushed ahead, his legs pumping faster and faster.

His quarry hadn't yet made it to the end of the block. In fact, he was slowing to a fast walk.

Why? Frank wondered. Then he saw it. A bus had pulled to a stop, and the guy was the only one getting on.

Frank shouted, "Wait!" and rushed up to the bus. It was too late. The doors were closed, and the bus was pulling away. Frank saw his quarry press close to a window and give him a mocking grin.

Frank leaned over and rested his hands on his knees, breathing hard. He scanned the street, frantically looking for a cab. He could follow the bus, he thought. It wasn't over yet.

But there was no sign of a taxi. Frank stood on the corner for five minutes, alternately staring down the street and searching for a cab.

Finally he gave up. The saboteur was gone.

Dejected, Frank made his way back to the train station, hoping that Nancy or Greg Ashby had had some luck.

His pace picked up when he spotted Paul Fox hurrying away from their train.

"Paul!" Frank shouted. This was his chance to interrogate Paul about Joe's disappearance. "Can I talk to you for a second?"

Paul stopped and turned back. He waited for Frank to catch up with him.

Frank jogged up to the actor. "Thanks for stopping—" he began, but Paul cut him off.

"Just what are you trying to do to me?" he demanded, his voice harsh with rage. "What did I ever do to you that you want to ruin my career?"

"Huh?" Frank took a step backward, dumbfounded. "Me, ruin your career? What are you talking about?"

"Don't tell me you don't know what I mean," Paul snarled. "First Kate—and now you've got that overzealous cop breathing down my neck, telling me that your brother has vanished and *I'm* responsible!"

"Whoa. Back up," Frank said. So Ashby had already interviewed Paul about Joe's disappearance.

"So you don't know anything about Joe's disappearance?" Frank said, eyeing Paul narrowly.

Paul took a deep breath. "No. I didn't even know he was missing until that clown Ashby accosted me this morning," he explained. "And by the way, I do have an alibi, as you mystery people say, for the relevant times."

"Oh?" Frank asked.

"Yes—sorry to burst your bubble." Paul's nostrils flared. "With witnesses and everything. I didn't go on the tour yesterday because I went to meet an old friend who moved to Salt Lake City. I left about ten minutes after the bus, and I didn't get back until the train was about to pull out of the station."

Frank pursed his lips thoughtfully. It was likely that Paul was telling the truth—an alibi like that would be pretty easy to check. Ashby *would* check it, too.

"Well, I guess you're off the hook, then—as far as my brother's disappearance goes," Frank said in a mild voice. Then, abruptly, he barked out, "But we do know you left that anonymous note accusing Joe of being involved in Kate's disappearance." He wanted to see if he could catch Paul off guard.

He succeeded. Paul blanched for a moment before deciding to tough it out. "So?" he said, sneering. "That's no crime."

"No, not in itself," Frank acknowledged. "But it does make us very curious as to how much *you* know about where Kate is. You're at the top of Ashby's suspect list for that one."

"Me?" Paul's jaw dropped. His look of surprise was comical. Frank thought, either he's one great actor, or this is really news to him.

"You can't be serious. I'm the one who told

everyone she was missing," Paul objected after a moment.

"You could have done that to divert suspicion from yourself," Frank pointed out.

"But"—Paul seemed truly alarmed—"why would *I* want to get rid of Kate? She's my scene partner."

"She's also competition," Frank said. "You're both trying to get a super Hollywood agent to represent you. He may not be able to take on both of you."

Paul gave a queer little laugh and closed his eyes for a second. "This is like a bad dream," he muttered, half to himself.

"What is?" Frank asked.

Paul opened his eyes and gazed wearily at Frank. "Okay, I guess it's time for the truth," he said.

Frank crossed his arms. "That would be nice," he said in a neutral voice.

"I never told her this, but I need Kate for that audition," Paul confessed. He took a deep breath. "The only reason we got the chance to do it at all is because one of Isaacs's scouts saw Kate in a show in Chicago and loved her. I've been helping to manage her career, so this guy asked if I could get her out to Hollywood." He shrugged. "It was a golden opportunity. I set it up so that she'd audition with a scene that needed a partner."

"Well, you still have the audition, don't you?" Frank asked.

Paul shook his head vehemently. "That's just it—I *don't* have the audition. I called Isaacs's office this morning and told them that Kate couldn't make it. He told me not to bother coming unless she was with me." Paul raised his hands in a gesture of futility. "So you see, I have a very good reason for wanting Kate to be found."

Frank found Paul's self-absorption a little repulsive, but he had to admit that the actor was right. He didn't seem like a likely candidate for Kate's kidnapper. Or Joe's.

Which brought Frank back to the saboteur. That guy was the only suspect left. But Frank had lost him, and there was no telling where he was now. Or what he had done with Joe.

With a mumbled apology to Paul, Frank climbed back on the train. He was feeling distinctly depressed.

"Just what are we looking for?" Bess wanted to know as Nancy led the way through the main branch of the Reno Public Library.

Nancy glanced up at the library's vaulted ceiling. She wondered if she was leading them on a wild-goose chase. But, no, if the diamond thief had been looking for information on Jake Comstock, that's what they had to do, too.

174

"Let's talk for a moment," Everett said, pulling out his handkerchief and mopping his face. He led them over to a set of curved wooden benches along one wall.

"I spent most of the night thinking about this," he said. "After Ashby told us that the Mastermind was out of the picture, I decided, okay, back to basics."

"So what are the basics?" Bess asked him, blowing a curl out of her face.

"Ah, I'll bet Nancy would like to answer that one," Everett said hastily.

Nancy suspected Everett didn't have a clue to what the basics were. He needed her to bail him out.

She narrowed her eyes. "The thief was probably investigating Jake Comstock," she said. "All we know is that there was something he needed to know or something he had to find. I'm beginning to think the thief didn't hide the diamond along this route—he took this way for a different reason."

Everett beamed. "My thoughts precisely!"

"So where should we start?" Nancy asked. "We don't have much time." She checked her watch. It was almost one. "The train leaves at two."

"What do you know so far about Jake Comstock?" Everett asked Nancy.

Nancy blew out her breath. "Not much. In

Central City we found out that Jake may have left his heirs the claim to a mother lode of gold—only no one knows where the mine is," she said. "I keep coming back to that idea. If there really is a gold mine, it has to be worth an awful lot of money, and since the thief probably knew a lot about Jake Comstock, maybe he was looking for the claim."

"Then why steal the diamond?" Everett objected. "A gold mine is worth a lot more. And the guy could have risked everything if he got caught stealing the diamond."

Nancy frowned. "I know. That part doesn't quite make sense," she admitted.

"I think Jake was a little crazy," Bess announced. "He sounds weird—he carried around a pretty expensive diamond as a good luck charm, he found a million-dollar gold vein and never mined it—"

Everett took up the theme enthusiastically. "Yeah—and didn't Jack say that Jake finally had the Comstock Diamond cut into the shape of a pyramid? Maybe Jake joined a bizarre cult. I'll bet if you looked up his will, you'd find he left all his money to the Temple of Isis, or something like that."

Nancy stood up abruptly. "You two just gave me an idea," she said, leading them across the library's marble lobby to the circulation desk.

While they were waiting for the librarian to finish checking out some books, Bess looked at Nancy. "You want to let us in on this idea we gave you?" she asked.

Nancy drummed her fingers on the circulation desk. "Genealogy," she said shortly, trying to catch the librarian's eye.

Bess stared. "What?" she asked.

Everett looked thoroughly puzzled. "You mean, trace Jake Comstock's descendants?"

"Right!" Nancy declared. "Maybe we can get more of a lead on this alleged gold claim by finding out who Jake's heirs were. If there are any Comstocks still living, we could contact them and see if they know anything about it."

"Hey, that's good," Everett said approvingly.

"How are we going to do it?" Bess asked.

"There's a library of genealogical information in Salt Lake City," Everett offered.

"That was what I had in mind. Do you think this library is hooked into it by computer?" Nancy asked anxiously.

"Only one way to find out," Everett replied as the librarian came over to them.

"Can I help you?" he asked, staring at the three of them over the top of his glasses.

Everett introduced himself, Nancy, and Bess. "Jared Sanford," the librarian said, shaking Everett's hand. "What can I do for you?"

"We have a favor to ask," Nancy said. "We need to find out everything we can about a forty-niner named Jake Comstock. Do you have a computer that can access the genealogical data base in Salt Lake City?"

"We do," Sanford said, "but I don't know that it'll give you much useful information. All the genealogical data base tells you is who a person's ancestors and descendants were."

Nancy nodded. "That's a start. Can we give it a try?"

Sanford led them to a room behind the circulation desk. There he sat down at a computer terminal and tapped out a few keystrokes. Nancy watched over his shoulder as he worked.

"Comstock settled in San Francisco," Everett told him. "We're not sure when he died, but it was probably around the turn of the century."

Nancy felt her hopes rising as Sanford typed the name. A series of names with codes alongside them appeared on the computer screen.

"Let's see," Sanford said, tapping out another series of keystrokes. "Jake Comstock. Died in San Francisco."

"That's him!" Bess cried.

Sanford hit the Print command. In a second the printer next to the computer was humming

178

away. When it was done, Sanford reached over and ripped off a sheet.

"This is all there is," he told them. "I hope it's a help."

Everett snatched the paper from Sanford and scanned it. When he finished, his eyes were gleaming. "Read this," he told Nancy.

"What is it?" Nancy asked, taking the printout from Everett. Bess leaned over to read along with her.

Nancy glanced through the report, which was a computer-drawn family tree listing Jake's descendants and their families.

It wasn't until Nancy got to the end of the report that she realized what Everett had meant. Jake Comstock had only two living direct descendants. One of them was a man named Stan Leighton.

The other was Laurie Adams!

Chapter

Nineteen

I KNEW IT! Didn't I say Jake Comstock reminded me of someone?" Bess was saying. "It was Laurie Adams. But who would have guessed?"

"The question is, is she keeping it a secret on purpose?" Nancy wondered aloud. "I think she must be. But why?"

Nancy, Frank, Bess, and Everett were back in Nancy and Bess's compartment. The train was heading west through the desert to California.

"There's a lot Laurie hasn't told us," Frank said.

Everett leaned back in his seat with his legs stretched out in front of him. "I think it would be a big mistake to confront her now. Let's see what else we can find out before we do."

Nancy sighed. Ever since they'd learned that Laurie was related to Jake Comstock, she'd been torn. There hadn't been time in Reno to do any more research. They'd had to rush back to the station to catch the train as it was. Now they were stuck. They knew that Laurie had been holding out on them—but that didn't necessarily mean she was guilty of any crime.

Except there was something about Laurie that was nagging at Nancy. What was it?

"We also need to find out who Stan Leighton is," Frank added. "The report the librarian gave you said he's Laurie's cousin. Does she know him? How does he figure in all this?"

"We'll do a check on both of them in Sacramento," Everett said. "We should be there in about an hour. We just have to sit tight until then."

"And make sure Laurie doesn't know we know about Jake Comstock," Bess added.

"How much time do we have in Sacramento?" Frank asked Everett. It wasn't one of the mystery train's scheduled stops. They were just pulling in there while the engine was switched.

Everett waved a hand. "Don't worry—we need only a couple of minutes to get to the police station. Luckily, I have a contact there who owes me a favor. I wired him from Reno to get us any information in the FBI files about both Stan Leighton and Laurie Adams."

"I wish I knew what Laurie was up to," Nancy said after a minute. "I just can't figure what the connection is between all these separate facts." She looked at Frank. "Do you have any brilliant ideas, Frank?" she asked.

Frank, who was preoccupied, started slightly. "Who, me?" he asked. Then he sighed. "I'm sorry, Nancy, I can't really think straight right now."

"Joe's fine, I'm sure of it," Bess said timidly.

"We'll find your brother, Frank," Everett put in. "And that guy you saw back at the station. Ashby's got the Reno police looking for him. They'll turn something up. And I bet when they find the guy, they'll find Joe, too."

Nancy was only half listening to Everett. She stared out the window and watched the sun glow over the desert. Jake Comstock's claim. The diamond. Laurie Adams. She remembered talking to Laurie in her compartment the night Laurie gave her the map.

Was Laurie reluctant to give her the map because she knew it held an important clue? So far, Laurie had hidden a lot from them. Was there something in the map she was hiding, too?

Nancy remembered how cagey Laurie had been about the other papers in her compartment. She thought back, trying to remember if she had seen something else among the papers on Laurie's desk. Then an idea came to her.

"His will!" Nancy found herself saying. "Maybe that was Jake Comstock's will I saw!"

"What are you talking about?" Frank asked.

"The night Laurie gave me the map, I saw a copy of some kind of legal paper tucked in with Laurie's other papers," Nancy said, her excitement mounting. "It had the name Comstock on it. I asked her if it had anything to do with Jake, and she denied it. She said it had nothing to do with our case, that it was part of her research for a book on the San Francisco Comstocks. But now I'm ready to bet she was lying. I think it was Jake's will."

"So?" Bess asked. "So Laurie has a copy of Jake's will. What does it mean?"

"Maybe it says she gets to inherit the Comstock Diamond," Bess theorized.

"But if she's the rightful heir, why would she put in an anonymous bid for it at auction?" Nancy objected. "No, I think there must be something else."

Frank was leaning forward now, as excited as Nancy. "What else did Jake leave to his heirs?" he asked with a glint in his eye.

"The mining claim!" Nancy and Everett said in unison. Frank and Bess laughed.

Everett smiled at Nancy. "Brilliant minds think alike, eh?" he asked. "Okay. So maybe Laurie is on the trail of the claim. Maybe it's even legally hers, since it's been handed down in the family. But we're still stuck with the fact that she's never told anyone on the trip about all this. Why hide the fact?"

"If only we could get a look at that will," Nancy said.

Connie checked his watch. "Fifteen minutes and we'll be in Sacramento. You kids want to come with me to the police station?"

"Are you kidding?" Frank asked with a laugh. "And miss the major break in this case?"

Nancy stood up. "That doesn't give us any time to look at the will, does it?" she asked.

Frank shook his head. "Besides, what are you going to do—ask Laurie if you could take a peek at it? We don't want her to know you're at all suspicious of her."

Nancy put her hands in the pockets of her jeans. "I guess you're right."

"Nancy," Bess said. "I recognize that look."

"What look?" Nancy asked, her eyes widening innocently.

"You want to sneak into Laurie's compartment, don't you?" Bess said, confronting her.

Before Nancy could answer, Everett was on his feet. "I think it's a great idea. I like the way you think, Nancy," he told her, giving her a slap on the back. "But it'll have to wait until we get back. Besides, we'll have more information then."

Nancy agreed reluctantly. Everett was right —they'd have more time later. Besides, Nancy would have to wait until Jack and Laurie were out of their compartment, and she didn't know when that would be.

When the train pulled into the station in Sacramento, Nancy, Frank, Bess, and Everett were the first off. In about five minutes they were pulling up in front of the one-story police station.

"We're here to see Quentin Lee," Everett told the day sergeant at the front desk. She buzzed Lee on the intercom, and a minute later a short, burly man with gray hair greeted Everett.

"Connie! Great to see you," he said, giving Everett a vigorous handshake. "It's been at least ten years."

"Since I was researching that book on the

vineyard wars," Everett said, returning his shake. "You were a big help then, Quentin. The book kind of flopped, but that's how it is."

"Hey," Lee said, standing back, "I still have my autographed copy."

Everett quickly introduced Nancy, Frank, and Bess. "Do you have any news for us?" Nancy wanted to know.

Lee ushered them into his small office. It was cluttered with police reports and computer printouts. He scattered a few of the papers and held one out. "I hope this helps," he said. "It just came in."

Nancy took the paper from him. Everett, Frank, and Bess leaned in and read over her shoulder.

"No record on Laurie Adams," Nancy said, reading aloud. "But here's something interesting about Stan Leighton."

"What is it, Nancy?" Bess asked, leaning closer.

"It says that Stan Leighton was in prison for robbing the Comstock Bank and Trust," Nancy said, her voice trembling with excitement.

"Was?" Frank asked, looking down at her.

Nancy met his glance. "He was paroled this afternoon. He's out now!"

Chapter

Twenty

JOE HARDY felt a dull throbbing in his temples and gingerly opened one eye. A bank of tiny green lights glowed in the air in front of him, casting a dull illumination. He tried to call out but couldn't. His mouth seemed to be covered with tape of some sort. A gag?

As his eyes adjusted, he realized where he was. The electrical closet. Knocked out. Kate.

Kate! Joe scanned the dim cubicle. A still, dark form lay on the floor beside him. For a second he feared the worst, but then he heard her breathing. She was all right—just out cold.

Under him Joe felt the rocking movement of

the train. Wincing at the effort, he pulled himself up from a lying position on the floor.

His legs were tied together tightly at the ankles, leaving him unable to move. He twisted his head around to see that the same strong cord bound his wrists behind his back. A glance at Kate told him she was firmly tied up, too.

The memory of finding her came back to Joe. Who had knocked him cold and tied him up and left him here?

Besides the train crew, he had seen only Jack Lerner on the train. Joe frowned, puzzled. Did that mean that Jack had knocked him out? It made no sense. Joe wished his head didn't hurt so much. It would be much easier to think if his brain weren't throbbing so.

First things first. Inching over to the electrical panel, Joe scraped his cheek along the row of switches, trying to peel off the wide strip of duct tape that covered his mouth. A protruding metal corner scratched him, and he groaned softly. Oh, well, no pain, no gain.

It took a few minutes, but at last Joe managed to snag the silver tape on the sharp piece of metal. He slowly pulled away, stoically ignoring the feeling that the tape was peeling off his top layer of skin. At last his mouth was free. He flexed his jaw, grimacing.

Next to him Kate moaned softly.

"Kate," Joe whispered. "It's me, Joe. I'm here with you."

"Mmmph!" She sounded agitated.

"Lie still for a second—I'm going to try to peel off your gag with my teeth," he told her. Maneuvering himself to his knees, he bent down and nuzzled her soft cheek with his mouth. He could feel himself blushing violently in the dark. "Sorry about this," he muttered.

Luckily for him, it was pretty easy to catch the corner of the piece of tape in his teeth. Joe clenched his teeth and reared back. The tape peeled off with a ripping sound, and he heard Kate's muffled squeak of pain.

"Sorry, sorry," he apologized again. Some hero he was turning out to be!

"Joe? Is that really you?" came Kate's voice. "How did you get here?"

"I found you," Joe explained, "but as soon as I did I was knocked out cold."

"Jack," Kate whispered.

"So it was him!" Joe cried in a hoarse voice. "He's the one who did all this?"

Joe could see the glimmer of Kate's eyes as she nodded. He wriggled into a more comfortable position. "Start at the beginning," he ordered Kate. "Tell me everything. What hap-

189

pened? What is Jack up to? Is Laurie in on it, too? Did anyone hurt you? Have you been here the whole time?"

Kate gave a groggy laugh. "Can I answer one question at a time?"

Joe laughed back. "Sorry. Take your time. It's just that I've—we've all been really worried about you." He rushed on, before she could think he was getting sentimental. "Just start with what happened after we came back from the trip to Emerald."

Kate struggled to a sitting position, then leaned back against the wall next to him. "After I left you," she said, "I was heading back to my compartment when I passed by Jack and Laurie's suite. Their door was open a little, and they were discussing something."

"What were they talking about?" Joe asked. "Can you remember?"

Kate nodded. "Jack was telling Laurie that they should have cut him in on it."

"Who?" Joe wanted to know. "On what?"

"I don't know." Kate sounded distressed. "All I know is Jack said, 'We should have cut him in on it.'"

"And then they saw you?" Joe asked. "They realized you had heard them?"

"Right," Kate confirmed. "Jack looked up and saw me in the hall. He knew I'd heard him. I denied it, but he didn't believe me."

"Then what happened?" Joe urged.

"They kept me locked in their suite at first, while they decided what to do with me. I was so scared!" Kate confessed, her voice trembling. "I tried to explain I had no idea what they'd been talking about, that I wouldn't tell anyone, but Jack told Laurie it was too risky to let me go."

Poor Kate! She had been through an awful experience. "Take it easy," Joe urged softly.

Finally Kate started speaking again, her voice no more than a whisper. "They moved me to an empty suite and kept me locked up there for, oh, I don't even know how long."

"That's where I found your pin!" Joe exclaimed. "The suite for the handicapped, down the hall from Jack and Laurie's."

"I hoped someone would find it," Kate told him. "It fell off, so I worked it down into the bedclothes. I was so glad they didn't find it when they made up the bed and moved me again."

"It was a lucky break," Joe admitted. "When I found that pin, I knew you were still on the train. Where did they take you next?"

"Here," Kate said, glancing up at the wall full of electrical wiring. "It's been so spooky. Laurie brings me food and takes me to the bathroom in the middle of the night when no one is around. I guess they'll be doing that with you, too," she added, sounding rueful.

"They never explained why they were holding you prisoner?" Joe asked.

Kate's only answer was a shrug.

Joe peered around the tiny room. "The first thing we have to do is get out of here. Then we can find out what Jack and Laurie are up to."

"How?" Kate asked. "We're both tied up, and the door is probably locked from the outside."

"Hey," Joe said, trying to sound lighthearted and optimistic, "I specialize in getting out of tight spots." He edged toward Kate, his back to her. "There's a pocketknife in my back pocket," he said. "If you turn around, so that we're back to back, do you think you can move your hand enough to pull it out?"

Kate squirmed around. Soon she had her back to Joe's. "I think so," she said.

Joe felt Kate's hands moving along his waist. Soon her fingers were at his back pocket. "Can you get it?" he asked.

Kate grunted. "Move a little to the right."

Joe did and felt Kate's hand reach into his pocket. "I've got it!" she cried. "Now what?"

"Now we saw our way out of these ropes," Joe told her over his shoulder.

"You've got to be kidding," Kate said. "That'll take forever!"

"Hey," Joe said, "I don't have to be any-where. Do you?"

"I hope this is okay," Frank said as Nancy opened her compartment door. He held out a tray of sandwiches. "The selection wasn't great."

Nancy closed the door behind him. "Did you see Jack or Laurie?" she wanted to know.

Frank nodded. "I told them Connie wanted to see them in half an hour in his compartment. They're going to meet you there," he told Everett.

"Good," Nancy said. "Did they ask why?"

Frank unwrapped a sandwich. "I told them that Connie was furiously working on a solution to where the diamond was hidden."

Bess giggled. "I can't wait to be there when they walk into our trap!"

Nancy held out her hand, and Frank passed her a sandwich. "It's not really a trap, Bess. Frank and I just want to know they're some-where else when we break into their compartment."

Frank sat down next to Everett. "Ready to spin them some yarns about the case?" he asked.

"Sure. Yarns are my business," Everett told Frank. "I'll keep 'em there all night!"

"Just keep them busy for a half hour or so,"

Nancy said, smiling. "Long enough so we can find out exactly what they're up to."

"And how Stan Leighton fits in," Frank added. "I can't believe it's just a coincidence that this trip has happened at the same time as his parole."

"I agree. You know," Nancy said, picking at the stale bread of her sandwich, "they're probably involved in some sort of race to find the diamond. I was just thinking about how hard Jack and Laurie fought to keep this trip going, and to keep it on schedule. Maybe Laurie was so set on this trip because she knew her cousin would be free in a few days and she didn't have much time to find the stone on her own."

"Hey!" Connie Everett jumped up. "This time I really have solved the mystery," he announced. "I know who stole the Comstock Diamond!"

Chapter

Twenty-One

"AGAIN?" BESS DEMANDED, looking skeptical. "I hope this guess is better than the last one."

"O ye of little faith," Connie chided her. He looked excited and pleased with himself. "This time I know I'm right."

"Okay, so let us in on it," Nancy said eagerly.

Connie spread out his hands. "What could be simpler? It had to be Stan Leighton."

"Huh?" Bess looked mystified.

"See, if Nancy's right about Laurie being in a rush to find the diamond before Stan got out of prison," Everett explained, "that must mean Stan knows how to get his hands on it. And why would he know that? Because he was the one who hid it in the first place!"

"I'll bet you're right! Good thinking, Connie," Nancy complimented him. He beamed.

"Okay, let me see if I understand this," Bess said slowly. "Stan Leighton stole the Comstock Diamond from Brigston's auction house fifteen years ago. Then he went on a trip that retraced the path of his ancestor Jake Comstock. We think he was looking for a gold mine—or the claim to a gold mine. He ended up in San Francisco, where he robbed a bank, got arrested, and went to jail for fourteen years." She shook her head. "That's just too weird!"

"It does raise a couple of questions," Frank agreed. "Like, why steal the Comstock Diamond? Sara Finney says it's not that valuable as just a diamond. It's valuable because of its history. You couldn't get that much for it on the black market, because you'd have to sell it without telling anyone what it really was. So why go to all the trouble of such a daring theft?"

"One thing is certain," Nancy said. "Laurie Adams wants that diamond. She got Brigston's to put up a reward for its return. Why?"

"Well, it's worth *something,*" Bess said.

"But it'll be returned to the auction house," Everett pointed out. "Laurie won't even be able to keep it."

Bess clutched her temples. "My head is spinning," she groaned.

"If both cousins want the diamond so badly, there *must* be something special about it," Frank muttered. Then he snapped his fingers. "Hey! Maybe it's a piece of a puzzle," he suggested.

Nancy stared at him. "What do you mean?" she asked. "What kind of puzzle?"

Frank waved his hands in the air. "I don't know, exactly," he said. "But it is cut in an unusual shape—a pyramidal prism. Maybe that's supposed to mean something."

"Like what? That Jake Comstock's mother lode is located in King Tut's tomb?" Connie asked, snorting.

Frank slumped back into his seat, frowning. "Okay, it is kind of far-out," he admitted.

Nancy checked her watch. "It's time to get moving," she said. "I just wish we knew a little more. I feel like we're so close to a solution."

"Not that close. We still haven't figured out who that guy is who's sabotaging the train," Frank reminded her. "Or where Joe and Kate are."

"We may be closer than you think," Nancy said. "I think Jack did recognize the saboteur when the guy attacked him in Chicago. He wouldn't admit it because he didn't want to have to explain why the guy was attacking him. So I think it's pretty safe to assume that the saboteur is also a part of this Stan Leighton–Laurie Adams thing. I'm hoping we'll find some clues in Jack and Laurie's compartment."

"Well, then, what are we waiting for?" Frank opened the door to Nancy and Bess's compartment. "We're pulling into San Francisco in less than twenty minutes," he said to Everett and Bess. "Go do your stuff. And whatever you do, don't let Jack and Laurie get off the train!"

"Good luck!" Everett said as he and Bess took off down the hall.

"Be careful," Nancy said quietly.

Frank put an arm around Nancy's shoulder and led the way down the hall in the opposite direction. "Don't worry about them," he said, "they'll be fine."

Within a few minutes, Frank and Nancy were at Jack and Laurie's compartment. Frank tried the door. It was locked, but Nancy reached in her pocket and silently handed him her lock-picking tools.

"That's what I like about you," Frank said, smiling at her. "You're always prepared."

As Frank turned the doorknob and pushed the door open, he felt the train slow down. He looked at Nancy, alarmed. "We must be coming into San Francisco early. Hurry!"

Frank stepped over to the pulldown table to check out a stack of papers. On top was a schedule of the trip. Underneath that he found the map that had been stolen from Nancy's compartment.

Nancy was at his side, also going through the papers. She frowned anxiously. "I don't see anything that looks like a will," she fretted.

"Maybe they hid it," Frank suggested. "Check their suitcases, why don't you?"

Nancy nodded and went to the closet. Frank returned to sorting through the papers.

The train was moving slower now. Then it came to a halt. Out the window Frank could see the station.

Quickly he ran his fingers through the pile. At the bottom he found a big manila envelope. Inside was an ancient-looking piece of paper. At the top, in fancy old script, it read "This Claim" in large capital letters. An old, hand-drawn contour map was paper-clipped to it.

"Check this out," he said, showing the contents of the envelope to Nancy.

"That might be what I saw," Nancy commented. "It was partly buried under some other papers. It looks like the deed to a mine."

Frank looked it over. It announced that whoever held the claim could take ownership of a mining stake found by Jake Comstock in the year 1852, in the Colorado Territory.

"It's the claim to the mother lode!" Frank nearly shouted. "So Laurie has it! I don't get this. Why is she chasing after the diamond when she has this claim?"

Nancy was peering into the envelope. She reached in and pulled out a yellowed slip of paper that had been caught in the crease at the bottom. She cast her eyes over it, then sucked in her breath sharply.

"Frank," she said, holding it out. It was a brief letter, written in a spindly script. "Read this."

Frank took it. " 'To Louise and Alfred,' " he read.

"Jake's grandchildren, if I remember the family tree correctly," Nancy put in.

Frank nodded and read on. " 'Here is the claim to the mining stake I once told you about. I am leaving it to you, as I know you are brave and adventurous children. I have devised a game for you. The stakes are high, so play wisely.

" 'As you will note, on the attached map there seems to be no mark to show exactly where my claim lies.' " Breaking off, Frank flipped to the map. "It's true, there is no mark," he commented. "Just some strange-looking contour lines."

"Read the last bit," Nancy urged him.

"'This is no error,'" Frank read. "'In fact, there is a mark—but you will find it only if you know how to look. The one who has my good luck will be the one who finds the gold.'" The letter ended abruptly there. It was signed "J. Comstock."

Frank stared at Nancy. "His 'good luck'— does he mean the diamond?" he asked.

Nancy's eyes gleamed with excitement. "What else? But the diamond was lost right after Jake died and wasn't found again until nearly fifteen years ago," she said.

Frank stared at Nancy. "So I was right," he said slowly. "The diamond *is* part of a puzzle. That's why Jake had it cut into such an odd shape. It must be a prism!"

"I think so," Nancy said, nodding. "I'll bet that if you place it at just the right spot on this map, it will bend the contour lines into some kind of mark that shows where the mother lode is."

"Wow!" Frank said. "That's why Laurie wants the diamond so badly."

"She had the claim," Nancy said, pointing to the paper in Frank's hand. "But she couldn't find the mine unless she had the key to the map!"

Frank dropped the paper and sat down on a nearby seat. "That explains a lot," he said.

"Why she organized this trip. Why she never admitted her connection to Jake Comstock. This wasn't just a fun trip to solve an old crime. For her and Jack it could lead to millions!"

"Stan Leighton must know about this, too," Nancy said, thinking aloud. "That's why he stole the diamond in the first place."

"Two cousins, each trying to get sole possession of Jake's mother lode. They must be greedy people," Frank said. "If only they had been willing to share, they could have had the money ages ago." He thought for a moment. "So what do we do now? We still don't know that what Jack and Laurie are up to is illegal. Devious, yes, but not illegal."

"Frank!" Nancy cried, staring past him and out the window of Jack and Laurie's compartment. "Look!" She pointed out the window.

Frank turned in his seat and pressed his face against the window. In a flash he saw what had gotten Nancy's attention.

Jack Lerner and Laurie Adams were standing outside on the train platform, looking right at Nancy and Frank!

Chapter

Twenty-Two

A**S SOON AS** Jack spotted Nancy and Frank, he grabbed Laurie's arm and yanked her down the platform.

Frank grabbed Nancy's hand. "Hurry! We can't lose them now!"

Nancy snatched up the copy of the claim. "I don't want this to get out of our hands," she explained. She followed Frank into the hallway. When she looked to the right, she saw Bess and Connie Everett running toward them.

"You guys!" Bess yelled. "Jack and Laurie got away! We tried to stop them, but they knew it was a setup."

Everett was standing next to her now. "I tried to stall them. I told them I thought the Mastermind angle wasn't dead. I was in the middle of giving them my explanation when Jack turned to Laurie and told her they were wasting their time."

"Jack's weird, Nancy," Bess said. "It was like—"

Before Bess could go on, Frank interrupted her. "Tell us later," he ordered. "Right now we have to follow Jack and Laurie. Let's go!"

Frank raced toward the exit, with Nancy, Bess, and Everett following close behind. Just as they were getting off the train, Nancy heard a voice calling out her name.

She turned around. It was Joe Hardy!

"Nancy! Frank!" he called out. He and Kate Harkins were running toward them. "Hold it! Where are you going?"

"I can't believe it!" Frank said. "Where have you been?"

Joe cracked a smile. "It's a long story. Where are you guys off to in such a hurry?"

"I'll fill you in on the way," Frank said, pulling on his brother's arm. "Come on—we need you!"

Nancy had raced down the platform and into the station, keeping her eyes peeled for any sign of Jack and Laurie. Then she found them.

In one corner a crowd had gathered, and Jack was in the center of it. He had squared off with a short man—the saboteur!

"There they are!" Nancy cried out. She darted in and out among waiting passengers and headed for the crowd.

Jack looked up and met Nancy's eyes. He didn't pause. He only grabbed Laurie's hand, and the two of them raced for the station exit, leaving the saboteur with his fists clenched.

Frank and Joe were at Nancy's side now. She pointed at the retreating figure of the saboteur. "Look!"

Frank shifted into action and started after the guy, Joe right behind him. Bess, Everett, and Kate ran up just then. "Go ahead!" Bess panted.

Nancy followed Joe and Frank out of the station. She spotted Jack and Laurie getting into a cab. The saboteur was trying to pull Jack out, but the train organizer managed to slam the door on him.

As soon as the saboteur saw Frank and Nancy, he took off at a run.

"What should we do—follow him or Jack and Laurie?" Nancy asked.

Frank hailed a cab. "We can't let Jack and Laurie get away. They're up to something big."

A taxi pulled up in front of them, and Frank ducked inside. Nancy and Joe jumped in after him, and Joe pulled the door shut behind them.

"Follow that cab!" he shouted to the driver. He pointed to the taxi that Jack and Laurie had taken and was now pulling out into traffic.

"No problem," the driver said cheerfully. The cab's tires squealed as the driver swerved around a parked car and pulled out of the station.

Nancy peered through the rear window to see Bess, Kate, and Everett hailing another cab. "They're coming," she said to Frank and Joe.

"The question is, where are we going?" Frank wondered as the cab left the station and merged into traffic.

"Looks like we're headed for San Francisco," the cab driver said. "This is the freeway that goes to the Bay Bridge."

"We're not in San Francisco?" Nancy asked.

"Nope," the driver confirmed. "The train stops in Oakland."

Dusk was settling in over San Francisco as Nancy, Frank, and Joe cruised over the Bay Bridge. Their cab driver was doing a good job of keeping up with Jack and Laurie's cab. "This is going to be some fare," he said over his shoulder as they got off the bridge. "I hope you kids are good for it."

"Don't worry," Nancy said. She turned to Joe. "What happened to you?" she asked.

"I found Kate, but Jack Lerner got me," he explained. "Jack and Laurie are the ones who kidnapped Kate. She heard them saying something about how they should have cut some guy in on it, and they nabbed her. Kept her locked up this whole time."

Frank let out a low whistle. "Who's the guy?"

"I'll bet they meant the saboteur," Nancy guessed. "He wanted in on their scam, but they wouldn't go for it. That must be what he and Jack fought about, back in Chicago."

"What scam?" Joe wanted to know.

Frank filled Joe in on what he and Nancy had discovered in Jack and Laurie's compartment. He pulled Jake Comstock's claim out of its envelope and showed it to Joe.

Nancy saw a look of recognition pass over Joe's face. "Yeah," he said. "I saw this in their compartment when I found the original of Machlin's map."

"The map?" Nancy asked. "Did they take it from my compartment?"

"I guess so," Joe acknowledged. "Right before Jack nabbed me, I was in his compartment. That's when I spotted the map. Jack said it had turned up, shoved under their door, but he didn't have time to tell you before you left the train at Kearns. I thought that sounded a little lame."

"Do you think they're leading us to the diamond?" Frank asked, staring ahead through the windshield. They were following Jack and Laurie through the hilly streets of San Francisco now.

"Either that or to Stan Leighton," Nancy said, nervously biting on her finger. "Or both."

"You want to fill me in on who Stan Leighton is?" Joe asked.

Nancy told him. "And he may have been the one who stole the diamond from Brigston's," she concluded.

"So Laurie's looking for him because he knows where the diamond is?" Joe asked.

"That's what we think," Frank agreed.

Jack and Laurie's cab made a hard right turn. Nancy and the Hardys' cab squealed as it followed. "They're taking the bridge," the driver informed them, sounding mildly puzzled. "Boy, these people are taking the scenic route."

Nancy saw they were headed for the entrance to the Golden Gate Bridge, which would lead them out of San Francisco again. A solid bank of fog was rolling across the bridge to meet them. "This is some ride!" Joe commented.

As soon as they crossed the bay, Jack and Laurie's cab took the first turnoff and screeched to a halt in a small parking lot. Nancy saw Jack race from the cab, with Laurie close behind.

"Come on!" Nancy shouted to Frank and Joe, quickly handing their driver some money.

Jack was climbing a steep hillside that went up from the parking lot. Laurie stumbled behind him. Nancy followed suit, making her way up on hands and knees when it got really steep.

When she got to the top, Nancy saw they were on a bluff overlooking the fog-shrouded bay. Nancy darted back and forth, searching for any sign of Jack and Laurie. She was having trouble seeing in the growing darkness, though. To make matters worse, the thick white fog was steadily creeping up the hillside.

"Over there!" Frank said, pointing toward the edge of the bluff. Jack Lerner was crouched down, digging with his hands in the ground at the base of an old oak tree. Laurie was kneeling beside him. As Nancy looked, a tendril of fog floated across her line of vision.

Frank raced toward Jack, with Joe and Nancy close behind. When they were about ten feet away, Jack rose to his feet. His eyes glittered with triumph. In his hands he held a small, mud-covered box.

"It's ours," he said to Laurie. "You were right." He looked at Nancy and the Hardys and laughed. "And there isn't a thing you can do about it," he told them.

Frank paused, unsure of how to proceed. "What should we do with them?" he called to Nancy.

Before Nancy could answer, a rasping male voice came out of the foggy darkness. "You can leave them to me—I know what to do with them," it suggested.

"Stan!" Laurie gasped.

"Stan Leighton?" Nancy guessed. Her heart sank. She had a bad feeling about this meeting.

"None other," the voice said. A heavyset, balding man in a cheap-looking suit stepped out of the mist, a gun in his hand.

The saboteur from the train was close behind him, also holding a gun. He tipped an imaginary hat at Nancy and the Hardys. "We meet again," he said.

Stan Leighton's accomplice, of course, Nancy realized. But she hardly had time to think about that just then. Stan Leighton was still pointing his gun right at Laurie.

"Hand over the diamond and the claim, Laurie," he said. "Or else I'll be forced to shoot you."

Chapter

Twenty-Three

JACK TOOK a step forward, then froze as the gun barrel swung toward him. "Don't even think about it, Stan," he said through his teeth.

"Oh, so you have the diamond," Stan said, catching sight of the box. "Kamida, get it from him," he ordered the saboteur.

Kamida stepped forward and took the box from Jack's hands.

Joe inched closer to his brother. "It's two on five," he whispered to Frank. "I think we can take them."

Frank gave an almost imperceptible shake of his head. He wasn't ready to take the risk just yet. He wanted to see what the choices were.

They were all in a semicircle now, with Stan and Kamida holding their guns on them. "What's this about a claim?" Frank asked Stan.

Leighton glared at Frank. "Keep quiet," he warned. "This is between Laurie and me." He squared off with Jack. "You guys were stupid to double-cross me like that."

"Who double-crossed who?" Laurie cried. "You're the one who took off with the diamond."

Frank poked Joe in the side with his elbow. "So he is the thief!" he said softly.

Nancy leaned in toward Frank. "What did you do with the claim?" she whispered.

"It's tucked inside my shirt," Frank whispered back. He gave her a curious look. She had a plan, he could tell.

Nancy cleared her throat. "Maybe I can help," she said to Stan. "Since you've got the diamond, you'll be needing the claim, won't you?"

Stan looked at Nancy as if she were an insect. "What's it to you?" he asked suspiciously.

"I can tell you where it is, that's all," she answered levelly.

Laurie gasped. "You wouldn't," she said.

"So that's how it is." A slow grin spread

across Stan's face. "And what might you want in return, young lady?"

Nancy shrugged. "Not much. A few hundred thousand dollars—and some answers."

Stan guffawed. "I like that—healthy greed and healthy curiosity. What do you want to know?"

Kamida's eyes narrowed and he shifted his feet. "I don't like this, Leighton," he complained. "We're wasting time here. We can find the claim—let's just take care of these people and split."

Stan shook his head. "There's no hurry. Let's satisfy these kids' curiosity," he said sarcastically. "It's no skin off my nose."

Jack lunged for Stan, but Laurie held him back. "Don't," she begged.

"Let me help you out," Frank began. "Laurie's your cousin."

Stan nodded. "That's right. We'd been told this story about the diamond and the mining claim since we were kids. When the diamond turned up at Brigston's, Laurie had the idea to steal it and then go hunt for the claim." He bared his teeth at Laurie. "I didn't find out until it was too late that she was planning to double-cross me. She had already found the claim—she had had it all along."

"You're the one who took off on his own looking for the claim." Laurie spit out the words. "Would you have cut me in if you'd found it?"

"Did Laurie help you steal the diamond?" Nancy asked.

Laurie turned on Nancy. "Why—the nerve. What kind of person do you think I am?"

Kamida let out a booming laugh. "Of course she did. She and Leighton were like that," he said, holding up two crossed fingers. "Or so Leighton thought," he added. "Actually, she just wanted him to do the dirty work for her."

"Shut up!" Stan warned him, scowling. "I've changed my mind," he added, turning to Nancy. "I don't feel like talking about this." He leveled the gun at her. "Tell me where the claim is," he ordered. "I might let you live if you do."

"Nancy!" Suddenly Bess's voice rang out in the mist. "Where are you?"

Kamida turned around, and Stan gave a tiny start. That was all the advantage the Hardys needed.

Frank shot out his leg, sending Stan sprawling to the ground. His gun sailed out of his hand.

Frank was on him in a second. Out of the

corner of his eye, he saw Joe take Kamida in a flying tackle and noticed two things skip-leap out of Kamida's hand and over the edge of the bluff. The diamond, Joe knew, was now at the bottom of the bay along with Kamida's gun.

"Nancy—Laurie!" Frank cried, looking behind his shoulder as he wrestled with Stan. "She's getting away."

Frank had Stan pinned to the ground now, and watched as Nancy gave Laurie a sharp neck chop. The older woman sank to the ground, out cold. Next Nancy went after Jack.

By now, Joe had managed to knock Kamida to his knees. He sent a blow to the man's head that put the saboteur out like a light.

As soon as Joe saw that Kamida was out, he ran to help Nancy with Jack.

As Nancy and Joe raced down the hill, they could hear Jack stumbling through the mist ahead of them. Suddenly there was a solid thump.

"Oof!" came Connie Everett's voice. A second later Nancy and Joe nearly tripped over him. He was sprawling on the ground, his legs tangled up with Jack Lerner's. They must have collided. Bess and Kate were standing a few feet away, unsure of what to do.

"Let me up, you buffoon," Jack said furiously.

"Nice work, Connie," Nancy gasped. Joe threw himself on top of Jack and pinned him to the ground. Then he fished some bits of rope out of his pants pocket.

"This is for what you did to me and Kate," he said, and began to tie Jack's arms tightly behind him.

As soon as Jack was securely bound, the group led him back up the hill. Frank was waiting there, perched on top of Stan Leighton's unconscious frame. Laurie and Kamida lay nearby.

Connie spotted Stan's gun and picked it up. "I always wanted to round up the bad guys this way," he said with a grin. He turned to the culprits, who were groaning and stirring now. "Okay," he barked. "Let's get a move on!"

"You tell 'em, Connie," Bess cheered.

Nancy, Frank, and Joe looked at one another, grinning in silent congratulation. It was over. Jake Comstock's legacy had come to an end. His gold mine would remain hidden— unless someone accidentally stumbled upon it.

Later that night the group gathered for dinner in a banquet room at a restaurant along

Fisherman's Wharf. Jack, Laurie, Kamida, and Stan were safely in jail.

Sara Finney was beaming at the head of Nancy's table. Next to her Connie Everett was pulling the claws off a lobster, and on the other side of him Frank and Joe talked together in hushed tones. Paul Fox sat next to Kate, looking subdued. Earlier, he had apologized to Joe for trying to pin Kate's disappearance on him.

"It's hard to believe Laurie was in on the theft from the beginning," Bess said as she dipped a shrimp into lobster sauce.

Nancy picked up another shrimp and munched on it slowly. "She knew her bid would be too low. Stealing the diamond was the only way to get it."

"But she didn't want to do it herself," Frank pointed out. He took a sip of his soda.

"So she convinced Stan to do it. And then he took off with the diamond," Joe said, shaking his head. "I guess he thought that if Laurie didn't have the claim, he might be able to find it by doing research on Jake Comstock. That's what he was looking for the whole time. He never meant to hide the diamond."

"Laurie didn't know that for sure, though," Everett pointed out, wiping his hands on a napkin. "She had to check the whole route. I

217

take back what I said about Machlin," he added with a laugh. "The map wasn't even his work. Laurie was the one who put it together —it was all part of her hoax."

"Is that why she stole the map?" Bess wanted to know.

Nancy nodded. "I guess she didn't want us to suspect that it was a fake. She must have heard Connie asking to look at it. She thought he might recognize that the scribbles weren't Machlin's writing."

"And I would have, too," Everett boasted. "I think," he added quietly.

"I can't believe Laurie was looking for the diamond for the past fifteen years," Joe said, shaking his head. "It sure was a brilliant idea of her to organize this trip and use all of us to help her find it."

Kate reached out to squeeze Joe's hand. The two locked gazes until Bess's voice broke the spell.

"How did the saboteur fit in?" she asked.

Frank cleared his throat. "Apparently, Ron Kamida knew Stan Leighton in jail. That's how he learned that Stan had stolen the Comstock Diamond. Stan told Kamida he had stashed the diamond somewhere, until he could get his hands on the mining claim. When Kamida got out of jail, he went to Jack and

Laurie and told them about it. He wanted to be cut in on the deal, but they refused."

"So Kamida went back to Stan," Nancy explained, "and Stan told him *he* would cut Kamida in on the deal if he delayed Jack and Laurie's trip long enough for Stan to retrieve the diamond before anyone else found it."

Everett took a sip from his water glass. "What I don't understand is how Laurie figured out where the diamond was. She hadn't known for fifteen years."

"Apparently, that spot was a place where Laurie and Stan used to play when they were little. They had buried a pet dog there years ago. After looking every conceivable place, Laurie figured that Stan could have hidden the diamond there. She didn't know for sure, but it was a good last guess."

"Hey, let's not forget the fact that it's right by the *Golden* Gate Bridge!" Frank quipped.

Bess reached over to give him a mock punch on the arm. "I'm sorry this case is over," she said with a laugh. "But I'm not going to miss your lousy jokes, Frank Hardy."

"I'm just sorry we were all used," Sara said sadly. "If only I had known," she added.

"Hey," Everett said, pursing his lips. "Don't be sorry. The adventure we had makes it all worthwhile, believe me."

Nancy laughed out loud. "So what are you going to do next?" she asked him.

"Write a mystery," Everett said.

"About what?" Bess wanted to know.

A wide grin appeared across Everett's face. "A miner, of course," he said. "Whose name just happens to be Jake Comstock!"